WICKED WILDLIFE

A COZY CORGI MYSTERY

MILDRED ABBOTT

WINGS OF INK PUBLICATIONS, LLC

WICKED WILDLIFE

Mildred Abbott

for
Nancy Drew
Phryne Fisher
Julia South
and
Alastair Tyler

Cover, Logo, Chapter Heading Designer: A.J. Corza - SeeingStatic.com

Main Editor: Desi Chapman

2nd Editor: Ann Attwood

3rd Editor: Corrine Harris

Recipe and photo provided by: Rolling Pin Bakery, Denver, Co. - RollingPinBakeshop.com

Visit Mildred's Webpage: MildredAbbott.com

❀ Created with Vellum

Under the muted pastels of sunset, a high-pitched wail cut through the crisp air. Beside me, Watson issued a low grumble from his chest and stuffed his muzzle between my thigh and the picnic blanket. I scratched him on the top of his head, then tickled one of his foxlike ears. "If you're trying to block out the noise, you might want to bury these, not your nose."

Watson sat up with a chuff, cast me an annoyed expression, and waddled over to his favorite national park ranger. Well... actually one of his favorite people in the world in general. I doubted the park ranger aspect mattered to my grumpy little corgi.

"Here, is this what you need?" Leo Lopez took the tips of Watson's ears and gently folded the tips down.

Watson only looked up at him in adoration.

"If I tried that, he'd give me the cold shoulder for a week." I gestured toward the red bandanna tied around Watson's neck. "Of course, you get away with dressing him up as well. So what else is new?"

Leo simply grinned.

Another high-pitched wail made Watson wince again, and Katie, my best friend and business partner, elbowed me in the side before pointing. "Look!"

Leo and I both followed her gesture. The three of us—four, counting Watson—were spread out over a blanket on the far side of a meadow in Rocky Mountain National Park. Though no sun remained, the edges of the rugged snow-tipped Colorado mountains glistened with a soft dusty pink that transitioned to purple and then a deep blue, revealing the first few stars of the evening twinkling high above. A movement caught my attention at the base of the mountains. A bull elk stepped from the shadows of the pine forest and into the clearing, then lifted his head. The pink hue of sunset illuminated his crown of antlers, and a cloud of fog seemed to billow from his mouth as he elicited yet a third wail.

"I find it beautiful now, but the first time I heard it, I thought someone was getting murdered." Katie paused until the elk finished its cry. "Did you know what makes the elk's bugling sounds so strange is that they're actually whistling through their nose and roaring through their mouth at the same time?" She started to nod in satisfaction, then narrowed her gaze at Leo. "Of course *you* already knew that, Smokey Bear. Why do I even bother with animal trivia when you're around?"

He winked at her. "I can feign shock and surprise if you'd like me to."

"Oh, shut up." Katie chuckled and reached across me toward Leo. "Give me your mug. I'll fill up your hot chocolate. That is if Watson will allow you to free one of his ears for a second."

"Watson nearly went into hysterics when the bugling started last month. We were dead asleep, and then suddenly a couple of those ultrasonic wails happened right outside the bedroom. Pretty sure he thought we were going to be eaten alive." I chuckled at the memory of Watson, wide-eyed and pounding his tiny forepaws on the side of my bed, demanding that I wake up and take care of things. "The bugling season was over by the time we moved up here last year, so he'd never experienced it before. Honestly, it startled me as well. I hadn't heard it since I'd visited Estes Park as a kid."

The elk bugled again, silencing us. In truth, the sound was rather creepy—like a scream, whistle, and guttural groan, creating some otherworldly song—but also hauntingly beautiful. Especially combined with our majestic surroundings. Possibly it was my imagination, but there seemed to be a sadness in the tone. Maybe it was because I knew it was one of the last of the season. October only had one more day and like the few remaining gold leaves on the aspen trees, this would be one of the last elk calls until next autumn.

The three of us sat on our picnic blanket, huddled in sweaters and under other blankets against the growing chill, a hint of snow in the air. There'd been a slight lull in the tourist traffic between high summer, kids returning to school, and the couple of weeks surrounding the elk fest which took over Estes Park to celebrate the bugling season. Katie and I had been so busy at the Cozy Corgi Bookshop and Bakery that we had very few moments like this to relax and revel in the astoundingly beautiful place we called home and be with friends who were family.

As the elk disappeared back into the shadows of the forest, Leo glanced at me once more, his hand never stopping its caress over Watson's back. "I hadn't even realized. You and Watson have been in Estes Park a year now."

"Almost." I nodded. "We moved here last

November." That was a marvel as well. I looked between him and Katie, remembering the moment I'd met each of them. Katie, behind the candy counter of Sinful Bites, offering me chocolate, her smile wide and her hair frizzy. I should've known in that moment we'd be best friends. And then Watson and I meeting Leo as we'd entered the national park for the first time. I'd barely been able to string an intelligible sentence together at the sight of his ridiculously handsome face. A wave of gratitude swept over me, and I reached out from my place between them, patting each one on the knee. "I'm so glad Watson and I made the choice to move to Estes. I knew I wanted to be closer to family and open the bookshop, but I never dreamed I'd find..." My throat constricted taking away my words.

"Ahhh..." Katie wrapped an arm over my shoulders and pulled me close. "We love you too, you big sap." Despite her giggle, I caught the hint of emotion in her words as well.

Leo scooted closer so he could follow her gesture, putting his arm over Katie's and my shoulders and squishing Watson between his and my legs. Watson didn't even grumble. "It's true. We do. Honestly, I loved living here, loved my job, but I didn't really feel connected before you, hadn't quite been able to call it home. Then Winifred Page and her sidekick Watson showed up, and everything just clicked into place. Turns out you're the glue."

There was no chance I'd be able to speak after that.

"Glue?" Katie leaned forward so she could look around me. "Let's not call Fred glue. How about... icing? She's the icing that holds..." She shook her head. "No, that doesn't work." She slapped my thigh with her other hand. "Ice cream! She's the ice cream that holds the ice cream sandwich together." She grinned, then scowled, clearly dissatisfied.

Leo considered. "How about she's the binding that holds the book together."

"Now *that's* good. Perfect for our little bookseller." I could feel Katie pat Leo's arm over my shoulder. "Although, she could also be..." She snapped her fingers rapidly. "What's that envelope called in the Clue game? You know, the one where you put the cards of murderer, the weapon, and the room."

"I think it's called an envelope," Leo answered smugly.

"Well, whatever," Katie responded with another scowl, before looking at me. "That's another part you didn't anticipate when you moved to Estes, huh? That you'd become the resident Nancy Drew."

"You can say that again." Though I hadn't expected to discover such amazing friends, that aspect was much less surprising than the bevy of murders I'd stumbled across over the past year.

"Speaking of, it's been a little over a month since—"

"Don't you dare say it!" I smacked my hand over Leo's mouth with a laugh before he could finish that statement. "There's no reason to jinx anything."

He muttered something behind my hand and made a show of waggling his eyebrows.

Katie giggled and scooted away so it was easier to face us. "He has a point, Fred. Tomorrow is Halloween. It'd be a perfect night for murder."

Leo repositioned once more, so the three of us were spread out over the blanket again. "That may be true for most places, but Halloween in Estes is about the least scary thing I've ever seen. If there was any night to count on not getting murdered, I think Halloween is the one."

Watson remained at my side, lifting his head to make sure Leo was near but then drifting off again almost instantly.

"I like that answer." I pointed to Leo. "Let's go

with that. I'm looking forward to tomorrow night's celebration. A bunch of cute kids and pets in Halloween costumes wandering around downtown. It'll be fun. No murders needed."

"I agree." Katie shimmied happily. "Plus I have a new recipe I'm going to try out on everyone tomorrow. Can't have another murder take away from that." She considered. "Come to think of it, it's amazing how many of my recipes get overshadowed by murder."

"Katie, my dear, I've not seen a murder yet that can overshadow your baking." Leo smiled warmly at Katie, and for the millionth time I wondered if something much more than friendship was going on between my two best friends.

Katie shimmied again. "You know what, I can't disagree with you there." She grew serious. "Are you going to be able to make it down tomorrow?"

Leo shrugged. "I'm not really sure. Hopefully." He gestured toward the forest. "Depends on what happens."

I looked between them. "Why, what happened?"

Katie sucked in a breath, aghast. "Oh! I forgot to tell you." She gestured toward Leo but answered for him. "There was another poaching incident yesterday."

I turned from Katie to gape at Leo. "Seriously? How many is that this month?"

"Six. Another elk this time." All levity from the moments before fled his tone, and his expression became hard and angry, making him look more like a man in his early thirties than he normally did. "And the police are doing the bare minimum possible and say that it's because of our incompetence." He winced in way of apology at me. "You know I try not to say anything bad about Wexler, but... it's getting old."

Despite ending things with Sergeant Wexler months ago, I felt my cheeks heat at the mention of him. "I don't blame you. And I know you and Branson have never seen eye to eye on the poaching."

With a sigh, Leo shook his head, his anger transitioning to annoyance. "Of course, there're a few rangers who think it's just part of the job, that there's only so much we can do, so I can't put all the blame on the police force."

"At least you're not alone now. That new ranger..." Katie snapped her fingers again.

"Nadiya," Leo provided.

"Right!" Katie pointed at him like he'd just won a trivia game. "You said Nadiya is really taking it on as a cause, so you're not quite as alone in the fight like before."

"That's true. She is. But still..." He sighed and shook his head. "Sorry. I don't mean to ruin a good night. We haven't been able to do this in a while. No reason to make it depressing."

We were quiet for a minute, only the gentle breeze cutting through the branches and Watson's soft snores breaking the silence, until Katie giggled again.

Leo and I both gave her quizzical glances, which only made her giggle harder.

"I'm sorry! I really am. It's just that... It's awful that we were joking around about murderers a few seconds ago but then got all serious around the animals getting killed." She held up a hand toward Leo. "*Not* that poaching should be a laughing matter."

She had a point.

"You're right." Leo shrugged. "But there's something, for me at least, that gets to me about animals. Maybe it's because I'm a park ranger, but... animals don't ask for any of this. They're just going about their lives. We're the ones who intrude, the ones who hurt them. Granted, I'm not saying hunting is bad when done responsibly, *and* I'm not saying humans deserve to be murdered either, but...." He wrinkled his nose. "I don't know... people as a species get into all this drama and twists and turns and lies and secrets and all that jazz that goes behind murder a lot of the time. Animals don't do that."

"Tell that to Bambi."

I flinched and looked over at Katie at her unexpected comment, unable to hold back a laugh. "What?"

"Bambi." Katie looked between Leo and me as if the explanation should've been obvious. "When the bear ate Bambi's mother. Just saying, I don't think Bambi would've made a distinction between human drama and the bear being hungry. Either way his mother died."

"Katie, what weird non-Disney version of that film have you seen? A *hunter* killed Bambi's mom."

Katie narrowed her eyes at Leo, then looked to me for confirmation.

I nodded. "That's true."

"Really?" Katie tapped her chin. "Wonder what movie I'm thinking of? Maybe *Cujo*."

"*That* was about a killer dog, and most definitely *not* Disney. It was based on a book by Stephen King." I laughed again. "I have to say I'm surprised. After all this time, I never would've expected it. I thought the trivia queen knew everything. It seems you have an unusual gap in the movie knowledge category." Although, Katie had experienced a rather unusual childhood, so that might be an explanation.

His mood brightening, Leo stage-whispered in my direction. "Quick, let's go to your house, dig out Trivial Pursuit, and beat the trivia master while she's having an off night."

"None of that." Unamused, Katie straightened. "So movies aren't my strong point. I'd say that's a good thing. There're much more important things to do in life than stare at a screen all day."

I couldn't help myself. "Don't your frequent binges into the wormhole that is the Google search engine require a screen?"

Katie practically sputtered. "That's different! That's... educational!"

Leo and I both laughed and then laughed harder as Katie scowled. Between us, Watson gave an annoyed huff.

Leaning toward Katie, I grabbed her hand. "Oh, sweetie. We're just giving you a hard time. Honestly, I'm glad to know there's one area where you have a few gaps. I was starting to wonder if you were human at all, that maybe the government had installed some high-powered encyclopedic software in your brain and..." A light in the distance caught my attention, and I refocused on the forest, close to where the elk had bugled.

There was nothing there. I must've been seeing things.

Then another quick flash. I pointed toward it. "Look. There's something down there. Besides the animals, I mean. I could've sworn I just saw a flashlight."

Leo stiffened instantly and looked toward the forest.

Several moments passed, the night once more undisturbed by anything other than Watson's snores.

Just as I was about to decide I'd been wrong, it flashed again.

"Leo," Katie whispered. "Your poacher."

Leo sprang up, startling Watson awake, and started to rush back up the hill toward where we'd parked. "I left the walkie-talkie in the truck." He'd nearly reached the ranger vehicle when a gunshot sounded.

All four of us, Watson included, turned toward the sound in the dark forest.

Then Leo tore past us, nearly leaping over the blanket in his haste. Springing up, Watson was instantly on Leo's heels, and the two of them raced across the meadow.

Katie and I sat dumbfounded for a couple of heartbeats, then looked at each other. As one, we stood and began to follow.

"Leo! Stop!" Katie called after him as we ran.

Whether he heard and ignored her, or Katie's voice was lost over the crash of underbrush beneath our feet, I wasn't sure. Either way, he kept going.

The toe of my cowboy boot snagged on something and I stumbled. Katie reached out a hand, steadying me before I fell, and then we were off again.

By the time Katie and I were halfway across the meadow, Leo and Watson had disappeared into the darkness of the trees. Somewhere in the back of my mind, a voice yelled for me to calm down, to *slow* down. To take just a moment to figure out the right plan, because this wasn't it. Clearly. Whoever was in the forest had a gun. The most dangerous thing Leo, Katie, and I had was a corgi. And while Watson could turn being grumpy into an Olympic sport, he was hardly deadly.

Even so, nothing broke through the adrenaline of the moment and our crazed rush toward the trees or the pounding of the heartbeats and footfalls thudding in my ears.

Katie and I paused at the edge of the woods, unclear where Leo and Watson had gone. The only thing I could hear for a few moments was our combined panting breaths. After a few seconds, Katie pointed off toward the left. "There!"

With the gesture, I heard Leo and Watson crashing through the underbrush.

Katie and I took off again in their direction. For the first time, fear trickled in, past the adrenaline and the excitement of catching Leo's poacher. Because that's what it was—excitement. Fear for Leo and Watson eclipsed all of that, and the voice in the back of my head grew louder, screaming, *Gun! You're all running toward a person with a gun!*

Well, there was nothing to do about it then. I wasn't about to leave Leo or Watson alone. It didn't matter if I had no clue what I was going to do once I reached them. I continued our flight through the forest, still trying to think of options.

Pausing a couple more times to judge the sound of Leo and Watson's trajectory, Katie and I followed and came to a screeching halt as we discovered them in another clearing, this one barely more than five feet wide.

Leo knelt over the prone body of the bighorn sheep, a bullet wound in its side.

Watson nudged the sheep's nose with his own.

Leo looked up at us, his expression a mixture of grief and fury. "The poacher heard us coming, obviously, and ran."

Katie took a step forward. "The sheep, is it...?"

Leo looked down at the animal, running a hand lovingly over the curve of one of its twisting horns. "Dead. Whoever the guy is, he's a good shot at least. It was quick."

Watson whimpered and looked back at me.

Kate and I walked over, and I knelt beside them, putting my hand on Watson's back. "I don't think we should stay here. We need to—"

Sound broke through the night from far into the forest. All of us went rigid and looked into the darkness. It could have been the poacher, the elk, anything.

Leo stood, angling toward the noise.

I shot out my hand and grabbed his wrist. "Leo, no."

"Fred I've got to—" He started to jerk his arm away but stopped, his gaze flicking from me to Watson and to Katie. After a moment, his shoulders slumped. "I'm sorry. This was stupid. I shouldn't have... put you all in danger." With a nearly longing glance back toward the woods, Leo motioned the way we'd come. "Let's get out of here. I doubt the poacher is coming back. I'm sure he's not, but... whatever. Let's get to the truck, and I'll make the call."

"Oh my goodness, Fred! I thought Watson wouldn't wear outfits." Paulie gaped at my feet as he approached Katie's and my table outside of the Cozy Corgi. "Although, I'm not sure a bandanna qualifies as an outfit per se."

"I think it does. He's a cowboy." I decided not to let Paulie in on the secret that I hadn't taken off the bandanna since Leo had put it on Watson the night before.

"Then he needs a hat. I have one at Paws that should fit." Paulie gestured toward his pet shop across the street as his two corgis surged forward to greet Watson.

Watson let out the tiniest of growls, and the pair managed to calmly lick and sniff him, as calm as I'd ever seen them in any case.

"Feel free if you want to lose a hand." I smiled up

at Paulie as I knelt to pet Flotsam and Jetsam. Considering they were two of the most obnoxious dogs in the entire world, Watson and I had both grown rather fond of them. I paused as I took in their long green costumes that had a row of black felt running down their spines making it look like a mohawk. As they wriggled in their barely contained excitement at seeing Watson, their fabric tails wagged behind them. "They probably don't know what to do with themselves, since they're not used to having tails. What are they? Some sort of dinosaur or..." My words trailed off as the answer was obvious. "They are their namesakes. Flotsam and Jetsam, the eels from *The Little Mermaid*."

"Yep!" When I looked up, Paulie beamed, and only then did I notice his face was painted red, which highlighted his yellowed teeth. He leaned forward with a stage whisper. "I actually used these costumes two years ago, but they're just too cute to let go to waste."

"Can I pet your dogs?" A little girl dressed like a chipmunk didn't wait for a reply and reached for the corgis. Watson took shelter beneath my skirt while Flotsam and Jetsam lost control and bounced all over her.

The little girl's parents glared at me as if it was my fault.

Paulie didn't even notice. "That's my good boys. Show that little chipmunk how much you love her."

Within another couple of seconds, the father scooped up his daughter in his arms, and they hurried off toward another table.

Still oblivious, Paulie shifted his grin back to me. "I think this is my favorite night of the year in Estes." He gestured around the downtown. "All the store owners out in front of their shops, with the local families and some tourists wandering about, all eating and happy. It's almost like Christmas."

I snorted out a laugh, feeling a wave of affection for my odd friend. "Yes, Halloween is *just* like Christmas."

"Now that's a weird thing to say." Katie emerged from the front door of the Cozy Corgi with a tray of bakery items and plopped them on the table in front of me. "If Christmas is like Halloween, then you're doing one or both of them wrong." She grinned at Paulie, gave him a once-over, inspected the eel-corgis, and caught on instantly. "Very literal interpretation, Paulie." She pointed at his red-painted face. "Sebastian the crab?"

His smile broadened even further. "You got it. I

tried to talk Athena into dressing up like the little mermaid for me, but she wasn't going for it." His brown eyes went wide. "Athena! Oh, shoot! I left her manning my booth. I was supposed to get us some hot apple cider." He pointed all the way down toward the other block. "That's what they're serving at the toy store. I better go." He waved to Katie and me. "See you guys later! Come on, boys." He hurried off, dragging his two corgis behind him on their leashes as they attempted to jump on every person they passed.

"He's a hot mess, that one." Katie smiled after him, her voice communicating the same affection I felt for him, before turning her attention back to the food. "Here, try these. They just came out of the oven."

I did. On one side of the tray, there were buttery, golden brown bread balls, and on the other, bruschetta. I picked up one of the warm toasts piled with tomatoes, capers, and olives. The beautiful tang of garlic combined with the salty flavors over-whelmed me, and I glared at Katie, talking with my mouth full. "I hate you. I have no choice but to eat ten of these tonight." I took a second bite, finishing it off. "*At least* ten."

"Those are good. I have to admit." She beamed.

"It's a new bread recipe I'm trying. The dough is infused with garlic." She pointed to the balls. "These are the same recipe, but there's mozzarella and pizza sauce inside. Better than candy for all our trick-or-treaters."

I snagged one. *Homemade pizza balls! I love my life.*

"This is wonderful." Katie sighed as she inspected the downtown. "It just feels like this big, happy family." She chuckled. "Maybe that's what you meant by saying Halloween is just like Christmas."

I didn't correct her, instead taking in the sights and sounds around us. Despite the drama of the poaching incident from the night before, a peaceful feeling enveloped me.

Orange lights were strung over the two-block length of the downtown, creating a cheerful glow over the streets that had been shut down for the occasion. The shops, fashioned in a mixed typical 1960s mountain style and log cabin façades, were charming on a normal day, but with all the storeowners dressed up and handing out candy, toys, and souvenirs to the meandering hordes of trick-or-treaters, I couldn't help but feel that Estes Park had outdone itself. I supposed it hadn't, since it was a yearly event.

Judging from the ornate costumes that ranged from little children dressed up like animals to adults looking like they just came from a cosplay convention dressed as superheroes and comic book characters, I decided I needed to put a lot more thought into my outfit for next year. I'd donned a black broomstick skirt, black blouse, and black pointed hat and called myself a witch. Next to Katie, who'd dressed as Rainbow Brite, I appeared downright lazy.

"You look rather marvelous, if I haven't told you already."

"Thank you!" She tugged on the wig's blonde ponytail and gave a twirl. "Though I need to choose more wisely next year. I'm a little cold. I thought with these rainbow puff sleeves I'd be warm, but—" She gestured toward the blue miniskirt. "—brrr."

"At least the rainbow UGG boots you're wearing are toasty, I bet."

She started to reply, but then a fresh wave of trick-or-treaters and their parents swamped our table and began devouring the tray of bruschetta and pizza balls before moving on to the assortment of pumpkin scones and chocolate cupcakes, which were decorated on top with either fondant books or marzipan corgi heads. Katie had surpassed herself with the baking. I didn't know how she managed at all, but I was glad she did. The only thing I had to do all day was oversee the bookshop. Though, that had been enough. Katie and I had given the twin brothers who worked for us the day off to go to Denver, and with the influx of tourists for Halloween, we'd stayed rather busy.

"I say, don't these just look delicious!" Two large pumpkins walked up to our table, and the one with the female voice began shoveling scones and pizza balls into a large trick-or-treat bag. It took me a moment to recognize their faces, which had been painted orange and were peering from the cutout of the matching billowing fabric.

"Anna and Carl! Well, don't you two look completely adorable." I wasn't really sure *adorable* was the right word. Anna and Carl Hanson owned a high-end home décor shop across the street, and neither of them were petite on a normal day, but with both dressed as large round pumpkins, they were taking up nearly half the sidewalk and forcing a small group of ghosts and skeletons to give them a wide berth.

"Thank you, darling. We do, don't we? And you look..." Anna's gaze traveled over my witch outfit, and she was clearly unimpressed. Instead of finishing her statement, she focused on Katie and tilted her head in confusion. She probably wasn't familiar with the 1980s cartoon icon of Rainbow Brite. Giving up, she waved her hands in the air. "Where's my favorite little guy in the world?"

On cue, Watson emerged from under my skirt, knowing exactly what Anna Hanson had in mind.

"Oh my goodness, a scarf! You're the cutest little Frenchman in the whole entire universe, aren't you?" With a cry of pleasure, Anna started to bend down to pet him, but wasn't quite able to pull it off, given the round structure of her costume. Grimacing, she swatted at her husband and missed. "Carl, get Watson his treat."

Carl pulled his hand inside his pumpkin costume, rustled things around, and a few moments later pulled out a large dog bone that they'd bought from Katie a couple of days before. Knowing his role, he handed it to Anna. "Here you go. But I don't think he's a Frenchman, not with the pattern on the red. I think he's a cowboy."

"No one asked you for unsolicited input, Carl." She swiped the dog bone, made a second attempt to bend toward Watson, then ended up tossing it to him instead.

Showing atypical athletic skill, Watson caught it in midair, made a chuff that I hoped was his version of *thank you*, and disappeared under my skirt again.

Anna let out a satisfied sigh. "Sweet little thing." After a second, her smile faded as her gaze darted toward the windows of the shop to the right of the Cozy Corgi. "It's one thing for your brothers-in-law to be taking this long to open up their store, but the least they could have done was decorate for the occasion."

I nearly pointed out that the paper they'd covered the windows with was black so that sort of counted, but didn't. "They keep putting it off. You know Jonah and Noah—they get close to making a decision and then change it and have to alter the whole layout of the shop. It's been a couple of weeks since we've been allowed in to even help. I swear they're making mazes and trapdoors in that place." Despite meaning it as a joke, I wouldn't have been very surprised if that was exactly what they were doing.

Anna cast her scowl to the other side of the Cozy Corgi where my twin stepsisters were handing out crystal necklaces in small velvet bags in front of their new age shop, Chakras. "At least Verona and Zelda are making a go of it. Though I find their tie-dyed scarecrow window display utterly garish. It makes my eyes tired from staring at it across the street all day."

"Well, that'll teach you to stare, won't it?"

All four of us stiffened at Katie's comment, and from Katie's surprised expression, she'd clearly not meant to say the sentiment out loud. After a second, she cleared her throat and lifted what remained of the tray of garlicky bits of heaven. "Here. Take more of these. It's a new recipe. Let me know what you think. Your expert input of flavor is invaluable."

"Don't mind if I do!" Carl reached out and plucked up a bruschetta.

Slower to be persuaded, Anna gave Katie a narrowed-eyed stare for a couple more moments before leaning in, but not bothering to whisper. "I've been hoping to come over all day. But we've just been too busy. Rumor has it you were with Leo last night when the newest poaching incident happened." She leaned closer yet, and instead of growing quieter, got louder. "*And* rumor has it you were mere feet away from the *murderer* himself." Her volume spiked on the word murderer, clearly finding it delicious.

"I don't know if a poacher is considered a murderer or not." It seemed Katie couldn't help herself. Once more her eyes widened, and she held up the tray a little higher. "Here you go, take some more."

"A poacher is most *definitely* a murderer and should be treated as such." A sultry voice drew all our attention away from the food. An absolutely gorgeous woman with straight dark hair past her shoulders and flawless brown skin, stood a few feet away in a skintight pink bodysuit. She pushed her thin wire-rimmed glasses higher on her nose. "An eye for an eye is what I say."

We gaped at her, but I wasn't sure if it was because of her looks, her revealing outfit, or the fury in her tone.

"Goodness, breathe, darling, breathe." An equally gorgeous, though much taller, redheaded woman in a matching pink bodysuit nudged the first woman with her elbow. "There are no poachers here now." She smiled over at me. "Good to see you, Winifred. It's been a while. You never come in. You never visit." She smirked. "One would think you didn't approve of me."

On the other side of her, Anna sniffed and quite

literally lifted her nose in the air. "Can't imagine why."

Delilah Johnson was the owner of Old Tyme Photography, the shop that dressed tourists up in old-fashioned clothes and transferred their image onto tintype pictures. At forty-two, she was only a little older than me, my exact height, probably the same weight, but whereas I was full-featured and curvy, Delilah was pure sizzling centerfold. Nor did she bother downplaying the rumors of her being somewhat of a man-eater, whether the man was married or not.

At the sound of her voice, Watson popped his head from underneath my skirt once more.

Delilah knelt in one smooth, serpentine swivel and stroked Watson's head. "Well, Watson! Hello there, my handsome man."

Though he wasn't insanely head over heels in love with Delilah like he was with Leo, Watson pressed into Delilah's touch, and let out a satisfied groan.

I couldn't figure out my feelings for the woman. I didn't approve of her affairs with married men, and I found her somewhat abrasive. But on the other hand, maybe it was none of my business, and she'd taken what was easily my favorite photo of Watson and me.

Not to mention that Watson liked her, and that went a long, long way.

"What if someone hurt your dog? Wouldn't you want that evil person to be treated like a murderer?" The other woman looked between Katie and me and gestured toward Watson. "Surely you would want justice for him. Why should a wild animal have any less value?"

In my periphery, I noticed Katie, Anna, and Carl bristle at the idea of Watson being harmed. I did as well and felt my temperature rise. Though it wasn't explosive, my temper had been known to make me say things I later regretted, so I bit my tongue, trying to figure out what to say.

"Really, Nadiya!" Delilah gave a final stroke to Watson's head and stood. "You sound utterly unhinged. Don't say such horrible things about Watson, even in theory." And there she went, ever swinging the pendulum of how I felt for Delilah Johnson.

"I'm just saying that—"

"Nadiya!" Katie breathed out her name, just loud enough to draw all our attention. She blushed as our small group looked at her. After a moment she stuck out her hand. "You're Nadiya Hameed? The new park ranger who works with Leo, right?"

Though it took a second in coming, a friendly smile finally crossed Nadiya's face, making her even more beautiful as she shook hands. "I am. You must be Katie"—her dark gaze flicked to me—"and Fred. I've heard a lot about you. All wonderful things, of course."

Without realizing it was happening, I was shaking Nadiya's hand. "Nice to... ah... meet you." *This* was Leo's new park ranger?

I glanced at Katie, trying to judge her reaction to the stunning woman. If there was any spark of jealousy or worry about Leo and Nadiya working together, I couldn't see it. Maybe that meant there was nothing going on between my friends after all. That... or Katie was too well-adjusted to let it bother her.

"I do want to thank both of you for trying to help Leo last night. That's very brave of you to go after a poacher like that." As Nadiya released my hand, she pulled my attention back to her as her tone grew darker. "I only wish I would've been there. I should be in the park with him right now instead of—"

"No, no." Delilah shook a finger. "You promised Halloween to me, no work. Not tonight."

"Plus, I'd say it's lucky for the poacher you weren't." Carl nodded at Nadiya, clearly impressed with her ferocity, and his gaze traveled over the two women. "What are you supposed to be, exactly?"

Delilah turned and shook her hourglass rump in Carl's direction, a long pink tail waggling, which bopped Watson on the nose. It was enough to make him disappear once more. "We're the Pink Panthers, obviously. It's a new club I've started, but we don't normally take the dress code quite so literally." She turned back around with a wink.

Before he could respond, Anna snagged his hand. "Come on, Carl. We need to get back to our table. The tourists have probably robbed us clean." She dragged him back across the street without bothering with goodbyes.

Delilah chuckled as she watched them go, clearly enjoying the reaction she'd gotten. "That was fun."

And... with that, the sour taste was back in my mouth.

Nadiya rolled her eyes "And you call me unhinged." There was humor in her tone as she refocused on Katie and me. "Seriously, thank you. The world needs more people like you, willing to throw themselves in the line of fire to save our animal kindred."

"You're welcome, but, honestly, I think we were more trying to make sure Leo and Watson stayed safe." I didn't want a bighorn sheep to be killed any more than the next person, but neither was I going to throw myself in front of a bullet for one.

Katie shot me a glare that clearly told me to shut up. Delilah chuckled. "I really do like you, Fred. Your bluntness has its charms." She leaned back, looking over her shoulder before gesturing across the street in front of her shop to the three women manning the Old Tyme Photography table—each one of them in a matching skintight pink bodysuit. To my surprise, not all of them had the bodies of Barbie dolls or 1950s pinups. "You should consider joining our group. You'd make a wonderful Pink Panther." Her deep blue eyes glanced apologetically to Katie. "I'm not sure about you, Katie. Sorry. You're very sweet, but maybe a little too sweet. A Pink Panther needs some edge."

For the second time in a matter of moments, Katie bristled.

"Pink isn't really my color, Delilah." I couldn't keep the disdain out of my voice. "And I'd rather take the place of the bighorn sheep than wear a bodysuit." Realizing how that sounded, I gave an apologetic grimace toward Nadiya.

Delilah only chuckled. "See? There you go again." She shrugged. "Oh well. The bodysuit is just for Halloween, but pink is most definitely mandatory." She bent, stuck her hand under the hem of my skirt, and patted Watson. "See you later, handsome."

With that, she turned and walked away. With a dirty look—not that I could blame her after my bighorn sheep comment—Nadiya followed, her long pink tail sashaying in her wake.

"That woman has a serious problem," Katie fumed. "And is completely obsessed. Her softball team is called the Cougars, and now she's got a... I don't know... a *sorority* called Pink Panthers? She needs psychiatric help." Katie snagged a pizza ball and popped it in her mouth but didn't bother to stop speaking. "She also needs a few more pastries to take her down a peg or two. Although with her luck, it would probably only make her more *voluptuous* or whatever." She miraculously managed to convey a gagging noise without spraying any crumbs.

"Still, from the way Leo talks about Nadiya, it sounds like he's pretty impressed with her skills." I studied Katie for some sign, some reaction that would tell me if my suspicions were founded.

"Oh, what does he know? He likes Delilah too." She waved me off. "What man wouldn't?"

From what I could tell, Katie didn't seem to have any feelings about that at all. Maybe I'd been wrong.

Or... maybe I was the one who had feelings around Leo working alongside a woman like Nadiya Hameed.

And that thought made me want to take the place of the bighorn sheep as well. Good Lord! What in the world was wrong with me?

THREE

"Thanks for helping me carry everything up. It would've taken twice as long by myself." Katie popped another pizza ball in her mouth, then plucked a second off the tray and tossed it to Watson before leaning against the bakery counter.

For the second time in as many hours, Watson gave a surprisingly agile leap, snagged the morsel, and scampered off to sit under his favorite table in the bakery over by the corner window.

"Katie, we're business partners. You don't have to thank me for helping you pick up. And even if we weren't, you're my friend." I mimicked her stance from the other side of the counter so we were face-to-face. "Not to mention that you're going to be back here in a matter of hours." I glanced over her shoulder at the mess of pans in the kitchen. We'd spent the last fifteen minutes carrying supplies and leftover food from the sidewalk, through the book-store, and up to the bakery, but we hadn't started washing anything. "You sure you don't want to clean up?"

"Goodness no. Nick is coming in before school tomorrow to help me clean up and get the baking going for the day. I'm ready for that boy to graduate in December. Still so unfair that after all of his teacher's biases he still has to repeat this final semester." She groaned and sank a little bit closer to the countertop. "You know, I think I might just sleep here."

I patted her shoulder and straightened. "So you'll be complaining about having a crick in your neck all day tomorrow? No, thank you. Get yourself home and grab some sleep. I'd say the first Halloween of the Cozy Corgi was a success, and even if I never see another pink panther bodysuit again, it will be too soon."

"Success indeed! No murders!" Katie pushed herself into an upright position once more and dusted off the wrinkled shiny fabric of her outfit. "I'm going to agree with you about the Pink Panthers, though. I was so pleased with my Rainbow Brite idea, but next to them I just felt like an overgrown five-year-old." She grimaced and glanced at the tray of food once more and shoved an entire bruschetta into her mouth. "There. That makes me feel much better." Crumbs flying as she spoke, she held one out to me. "Take your medicine."

Laughing, I followed her advice, and at the savory butter-and-garlic tang, I did feel better.

After flicking a few switches and plunging the bakery into darkness, Katie, Watson, and I headed back into the bookshop.

"Actually, you know what?" Katie glanced over at me as we reached the bottom of the stairs but didn't wait for a response. "I don't feel bad at all about how many samples I had this evening or the ones I'm going to have to help me wake up in just a few hours. With as many trips up and down the steps as we've taken, we might as well have run a marathon."

"I don't know if your logic is sound, but I'm going to go with it." We'd left the overhead lights of the main level on the dimmest setting the whole night, so the warm wood tones of the floor and bookshelves glowed softly, soothingly. After the chaos of the evening, despite bordering on exhaustion, spending a few minutes alone in the Cozy Corgi sounded like a little bit of heaven. I paused at the door as Katie turned to lock up. "You know, I think Watson and I will hang out here for little bit."

Katie cocked an eyebrow. "You okay?"

"Yeah. I am." I bent down, ruffled Watsons fur, then motioned him back inside. "I think it's the whole 'coming up on a year' thing or whatever. I'm just feeling nostalgic, and grateful. Going to curl up in the mystery room and enjoy the reality of living my dream."

In a rare somber moment, Katie raised her hand and patted my cheek softly. "You do that. I'm so glad you are here. Not only because I got to open my dream bakery a lot sooner than I would've, but because you are my best friend and have made my life so much better." She offered Watson a similar gesture. "And you too, my hungry little fuzzball."

I locked the door after Katie left and paused, simply looking at the beautiful reality of my dream. The Cozy Corgi was so much better than I'd imagined, and I knew firsthand just how rare that event was in life. From the bakery upstairs and its myriad of heavenly smells and flavors permeating the air, to the picture-perfect bookshop that resembled a house with the main room in the center and smaller ones around the perimeter. It was a little slice of heaven, *my* slice of heaven. At my feet, Watson whimpered, staring longingly at the door. It seemed he was not having a sentimental moment and was ready to get home to his bed.

"Sorry, buddy. You're going to have to indulge your mama for a little bit."

Even though the lights were dim, with the large picture windows on either side of the door. I felt exposed to the night, so I flicked the switch and plunged us into darkness once more. With the moonlight and streetlamps, there was enough reflected glow to help me easily find my way to my favorite spot in the bookshop. I considered lighting a fire in the corner river rock fireplace of the mystery room, but didn't plan on being there very long. Instead, I flicked on the standing lamp, pulled a book at random off a shelf, and settled on the antique sofa.

Though his judgmental glare communicated that he was unhappy with this development, Watson acquiesced, trotted over and curled up by one of the carved feet of the sofa, and instantly fell asleep.

Without the fire, the light from the dusty purple portobello lampshade barely offered enough illumination to see the words on the page. It didn't matter. Much of the pleasure was simply sitting with the book, being surrounded by its fellows, feeling the pages beneath my fingertips and the comforting weight of it settled on my lap.

Even so, I scanned the lines through squinted eyes, none of it really sinking in as my mind wandered and my body grew heavy. When Watson's loud snores grew softer as he sank deeper into his doggy dreams, I began to be lulled to sleep as well. After closing the book, I reached up, pulled the tasseled string to turn off the lamp, and then rested my head on the puffy, recently reupholstered arm of the sofa and joined Watson in dreamland.

I woke, disoriented, not entirely sure where I was or even when it was. Not entirely certain why I'd woken at all.

There was a low rumble in the dark at my feet. Watson.

It came back to me in less than a matter of heart-beats. I was on the sofa in the bookshop and must've dozed off for a few minutes.

Watson let loose another rumble, a touch louder that time, nearly a growl.

I leaned toward him. "Watson, what's gotten—" A noise in the dark cut off my whisper and caused gooseflesh to break out over my arms.

For all I knew, it was the foundation of the old bookshop settling.

Even as the option flitted through my mind, some instinct told me differently. Sliding silently to the floor, I pulled Watson into my lap and wrapped my fingers gently over his muzzle.

Watson rumbled again.

I tightened my grip, not enough to hurt, just to communicate what I was afraid to say. Maybe he felt what I did, because despite hating being held or picked up, he didn't struggle. Though I could feel the rumble where my hand was pressed against his chest, he stayed silent.

There was another creak, faint enough that I couldn't tell where it came from—by the front door or above us in the bakery. Then another and another, followed by the unmistakable sound of a doorknob turning.

My overactive imagination went wild, picturing scenes from old horror movies I'd watched and moments from haunted-house books I'd read. From our spot on the floor at the edge of the sofa, I didn't have a great view of the rest of the shop. But my eyes had adjusted, and I could see clearly, thanks to the light filtering in through the windows. Nothing moved. No monster or villain was creeping toward us over the floors.

Watson's heartbeat against my hand brought me back to the moment, told me to quit being an idiot. Just as I decided to stand, to take action, there was a creak of a door followed by footsteps. Then a whisper.

"Yep. They're gone. The place is dark." Even as the voice spoke, it grew louder; though high-pitched, it was clearly male and unfamiliar. Enough so, between the voice and the sound of the doorknob, I now knew where it was coming from. I'd changed all the hardware in the shop except for the old brass knobs to the bathroom, the storage room, and the door that led to what had once been a crawl space but now was nearly big enough to qualify as a basement, filled with boxes of books and supplies for the Cozy Corgi. All three old handles were in the back of the store by the rear exit.

"Took them long enough." The second voice was deeper, softer. "'Course they probably left twenty minutes ago. I told you I heard them lock up."

I felt the rumbling growl build in Watson's chest again, and I gave another squeeze. He stopped.

"That's all we need. Running into the women who own this place." There was the sound of a door

closing and the twist of a door handle, followed by a
quiet curse and a grunt, then a click.

That settled it. They'd been in the basement.
That door never shut easily and required a push for
the latch to catch.

"I told you we should've waited until the whole
thing was done. But oh no, you *had* to come in while
everybody was still doing that stupid trick-or-treating
business outside. Couldn't wait for a sensible time."

"And I was right, wasn't I?" The higher voice
spoke again. "Nobody noticed—they were busy.
How was I supposed to know the whole thing was
almost over?"

My blood chilled at the implication. They'd
been down there while Katie and I made trip after
trip to the bakery. Though why it mattered, I wasn't
sure. Either way they were there right then. I tried
to think what to do. Being woken up in the dark left
me feeling completely unsettled. Much different
than if I'd opened the door and walked in on the
two men. Not being able to see them, not knowing
how big they were, if they were armed had me at
a loss.

Maybe they'd just empty the cash register and
leave. There wasn't much to steal in a bookshop and
a bakery. I couldn't imagine there was high demand

in the black market for the newest Nora Roberts book or a day-old cinnamon roll.

"What are you doing?" The man with the deeper voice sounded annoyed and a little farther away. "Let's get out of here."

"You going to give up? Just like that?" Higher Voice took on an apologetic and whiny quality. "I know I should've waited, but we've got time now. Nobody is here."

As the deeper voice started to speak, his footsteps creaked over the hardwood floor, and to my relief continued to sound farther away. Probably heading toward the backdoor. "There's no reason to look. All of Sid's supplies downstairs were gone. Just like I told you they'd be."

I jolted. *Sid? What in the world?* Sid had run a taxidermy business, Heads and Tails, in the building before I turned it into a bookshop. Below, he'd operated a grow house filled with marijuana plants.

"Maybe they moved them upstairs." The footsteps came closer, but I hoped he was walking toward the staircase.

"You're an idiot. A complete idiot. Obviously they got rid of everything." This time the other man's footsteps came toward the mystery room. "You're a complete screwup, Jim. I don't know why I bother with you. You lost the bighorn sheep last night and got us trapped in that storage room for an hour tonight. I'm about done with you. You're going to end up getting us killed, just like Sid and Eddie."

"What did you want me to do last night? I had no idea there was anybody around. Should I have shot that guy and his fat little dog? *Over a sheep?* I'm not a murderer, Max." For the first time, the higher-voiced man sounded irritated instead of pitiful. "There's a line, and I'm not going to cross it."

"Then you'll be the one who ends up dead." Again the footsteps came closer.

I was utterly frozen—both in terror and from shock. Sid, Eddie, the sheep. These two men were the poachers, in *my* shop, mere feet from me, and murderers or not, they were dangerous. And it sounded like only one of them had a problem with becoming a murderer.

"I say we check upstairs, maybe some of the plants are there. If so, this whole thing won't be a complete loss. Sid had enough to make a small fortune if we sold them to the right place."

"It's a *bakery*, Jim. You saw the women that own this place. Did either of them look like the type to stuff pot leaves inside a croissant or something. No! More like the 'stay at home with a book and pie on a

Saturday night' type." As he spoke, his footsteps drew nearer until finally large work boots came into view, followed by the rest of the deeper-voice man as he stood between the doorway to the mystery room and the front counter.

With my heart pounding, I pulled Watson closer to my chest, praying he didn't growl.

Though his rumbling never stopped against my hand, he didn't make a noise. But at my movement, I must have stroked him, causing a small cloud of corgi fur to float up and tickle my nose.

I had to bite the inside of my cheek to keep from sneezing or trying to blow it away with my breath.

The man matched his voice. He was huge, like two football players smashed into one. And from what the moonlight revealed of his profile, his nose looked like it had been smashed on several occasions, his jawline heavy and straight.

I prayed he wouldn't turn toward us. That was all it would take—if he just looked over his right shoulder, he'd see Watson and me cowering in the dark.

That wasn't how this was going down. I wasn't going to cower, wasn't going to be a victim.

Just as I started to release Watson and spring forward to catch the man off guard, he turned the other way and headed toward the counter. "Let's get the money and go." He paused at the cash register, looked toward the stairs and raised his voice. "*Now*, Jim. If you go upstairs, I'm leaving you. If you weren't my brother, I'd have left you already after your constant screwups."

The other man cursed, but I could hear his will deflating as he spoke. "Fine. I'll get the money. Then we'll check out the Green Munchies. It's still in business."

"Are you insane? You want to take produce from their store when Eddie isn't there? You really do have a death wish." The mountain of a man turned back to the cash register and opened it, then gave an approving laugh. "Not a complete waste of a night."

I'd not even thought about the cash register when Katie and I packed up. We'd done a couple thousand dollars' worth in cash that day but hadn't had time to run to the bank between closing hours and getting ready for the Halloween fest.

I couldn't care less. They could take it all, as long as they left.

Sid, Eddie, the Green Munchies? I thought my whole world was about to crumble. Or explode.

When the larger man slammed the cash register shut, Watson growled, bringing me fully back to the moment. I clinched my hands tight enough to cause him to squirm.

The man didn't look over. Watson's growl must've been much louder to my ears than in reality. Even so, I didn't loosen my grip. Every moment made it clearer than ever that any noise would've gotten us both killed.

A few more curses and grumbles and threats were exchanged between the men. A few seconds or minutes later—I wasn't sure—and they headed toward the back once more, and I heard the door click open, then shut.

We were alone.

Even so, I held Watson tight, straining my ears. After several more moments of silence, I released his muzzle and crushed him to me, burying my face in his fur in relief, gratitude, and terror.

Whimpering, Watson lavished my face with kisses.

I only gave in to the impulse for a few seconds before springing to my feet and rushing to where I'd left my purse under the counter. I yanked out my cell phone and dialed 911 as I hurried to the back door to make sure it was locked.

FOUR

If someone had told me there would come a time when I saw Susan Green's face and would want to break into tears of relief and throw my arms around her, I would've said they were insane. But when I unlocked the front door of the Cozy Corgi for Officer Green that was exactly what I felt. I stood back, giving her room to enter. "I'm so glad you're here. Thank you for coming."

Susan halted with one foot through the door, looking at me with a mixture of shock and repulsion. "Wow, you must really be in a state."

Even her grumpy response didn't lessen my inclination to give her a hug. Still, I refrained, waiting for her to come the rest of the way inside, and then shut and dead-bolted the door behind her.

Susan took out a notepad and pen before pausing to glare down at Watson, who offered his own glare in return and added a low rumble to boot. "Your ever present sidekick is... still ever present I see." She sniffed. "Oh, goody."

Even her disdain of Watson couldn't lessen my relief. "Their names were Jim and Max. They're brothers. And they were the poachers that killed the bighorn sheep. Or... one of them was at least. I'm not really sure about that." I launched in without preamble. The words gushing forth like a waterfall. I would've kept going if Susan didn't cut me off.

"Slow down. We'll get to the report part. On your call you said two men had broken into your shop, but you didn't realize it until you woke and they were coming up from your lower-level storeroom?"

"Yes, I already told that to dispatch when I called." There wasn't time for this. "I think they're heading to Lyons, to the Green Munchies. They said—"

"*I* said to slow down." She narrowed her eyes at me again. "What do you mean exactly that you didn't realize they were here until you woke? You were sleeping at your bookshop?"

I shot a quick gesture back toward the mystery room. "I was reading for a few minutes after Katie and I finished cleaning up from Halloween. I fell asleep."

She *tsked*. "Well... *that's* quite the exciting life you're living." She cocked her head. "I gotta give it to you, Winifred, you're playing the game with more skill than I would've anticipated. Did you even attempt to call him first?"

"Call wh—" I realized who before the word had even left my lips, but Susan jumped all over it.

"Don't play dumb. Your *boyfriend*. Obviously."

"Sergeant Wexler and I haven't dated in months, Susan. You know that." After feeling powerless during the break-in, it was almost a relief to feel my temper rise. "I didn't call *you,* for that matter either. You're simply the one dispatch sent over, or you saw that I was the one calling and decided to come over to make a stressful situation worse."

She smiled at that, like she was winning some sort of competition. "So you didn't even shoot him a text. Like I said. You're playing it well. Got him eating out of your hands."

"That doesn't even make sense. I had a break-in at my store, and I called the police. It's a *thing*—it's what people do. It's not some ploy to get Branson's attention. Or to have him eating out of my hands. We haven't dated in months. I'm not even sure if I'd call it dating or—" I had to shake my head to stop myself from talking. This was absolutely none of her business.

She studied me. "I almost believe you. I would, too, if it weren't working so well. I admit, most of the time, I'd enjoy seeing an arrogant man like Branson mooning over you from afar, but it's really just pathetic knowing that you're going to get exactly what you want. All while one minute playing the hapless victim, then the next acting like you're too good for him." She let out a dark chuckle. "Which, maybe you are. And that says something when I can't decide which one of you is more of a cliché."

Leave it to Susan Green to make me feel entirely like myself again, even if it was the version that had to replay my mother's words in my head to keep from saying things I might not truly regret later. I lowered my voice to keep better control. "Are you insinuating that I'm making all this up for attention?"

She started to speak, and I could see her lips forming a *yes*, but then she hesitated before letting out a long sigh. "No. No, I guess not. I definitely have your number, and while I don't like that particular number, I don't believe you'd lie about something like this, not even to jerk Branson around for your own enjoyment." She relaxed a little. "Sorry. Let's focus on the matter at hand."

I felt like I was the one being jerked around, getting insulted and apologized to in the same breath. But none of that mattered. None of it.

Before I could think of how to respond, Susan launched in again, her tone calm and professional. "All right, you said both when you called and now that you think the two intruders were the poachers. How do you..." Her pale blue eyes darted down to Watson, then back up to me. "Wait a minute. Did you check to make sure that they were gone?"

"I heard them leave. I locked the door behind them as soon as I called the police."

She rolled her eyes. "So the answer is *no*, you didn't. And here you keep pretending you're better than the professionals." She pulled her gun, and Watson growled. She shot him a glare. "Don't tempt me, fleabag."

"Susan, there's no reason to—"

She shot me a matching glare.

"Fine. *Officer* Green, there's no reason to search. They're gone." I started to take a step toward her but decided to stay where I was. I doubted Susan would actually shoot me, but I figured it was wise for neither one of us to have a loaded firearm in our hands around the other. Why push it? "Like I said, I think they're on their way to Lyons. We're just wasting time."

"Protocol, Ms. Page. Protocol." She lifted her chin. "Stay here while I secure the scene."

Maybe she was doing it for protocol—though she was several minutes too late—or maybe she was simply taking every opportunity to needle me further. I couldn't tell. Either way, I decided not to fight as she searched room to room and disappeared into the back.

I knelt and petted Watson with one hand as I fingered my cell phone with the other. Part of me wanted to call Katie, get her down here to have a friendly face. But it wasn't like she could do anything, and she needed her sleep. Same was true with my mom and stepfather.

As much as I hated to admit it, the real temptation was to call Branson. And not, like Susan suggested, to *jerk him back and forth*, but because I had no doubt he would take me seriously. He would've made sure I was safe and then headed down to Lyons to try to catch the intruders. At least I figured. There were times he was hot and cold, one minute telling me I did a better job at solving murders than some members of the police force, and the next telling me to keep my nose in my own business. But I didn't think there was a chance he would do that with this, not with what happened.

Part of me wished I'd gone ahead and called him to begin with. Then I wouldn't have been stuck with Susan. I supposed I could still call him, at least text. Try to convince him to not drop by the shop but head directly to Lyons. But as I considered it, Susan's taunts echoed in my head, and I let them get the best of me. I put the phone away.

"We can add anal-retentive to your list of irritating idiosyncrasies." Susan's voice sounded from the back, followed by a muttered curse as she struggled to get the door to the lower level closed. She rolled her eyes at me again from across the store as she emerged and headed toward the steps to the bakery. "You have your boxes of books and supplies labeled and alphabetized. Was that another fun Saturday evening for you?"

When I didn't respond, Susan slowed, almost looked disappointed, and then continued, gun still drawn, up the steps into the bakery.

Watson started to follow her, but I grabbed the edge of the red bandanna, and held him in place. "Oh no you don't. I know you're protective of where all your carbs come from, but we're not giving her a reason, not when she's got a gun in her hand."

He offered me a glare that rivaled the ones Susan had been doling out, but plopped back down with a grunt.

As Susan searched, thanks to her bringing in a sense of normality, no matter how irritating, I replayed some of the finer points of the intruders' conversation. Not only were they Leo's poachers, or at least two of them, but they had some connection to Sid and Eddie—which made absolutely no sense at all.

As I continued to stroke Watson, I realized it did, at least somewhat. Though Sid had already been murdered when I moved to Estes, thanks to Watson discovering a dead owl in the freezer in the back of the Cozy Corgi, it was revealed that he had been involved in poaching, or at least in the trafficking of poached animals. But Eddie... I couldn't imagine him hurting a fly. The young manager of the pot shop in the nearby town of Lyons had been a complete sweetheart. And the second in a long line of dead bodies I'd discovered since moving to town.

"All clear." Susan arrived at the base of the steps and headed back in our direction. I'd been so caught up in thought, I'd not even noticed her coming down the stairs. "Are you sure you didn't just hear things? There's no sign anyone was here at all, other than the money you claim was stolen. No footprints, nothing out of place. They didn't even take time to rearrange your alphabetized organizational system. Katie might have taken the money to deposit it in the morning, or, who knows, buy a cake from somewhere else. Maybe it was all a dream and you thought—"

A knock at the door caused me to jump and Watson to yelp, revealing we were both still on edge.

Proving that she wasn't, Susan simply steadied her stance and readied her firearm as she looked past Watson and me toward the front door. She lowered her weapon instantly and let out a curse that was almost too low to hear.

As I turned toward the sound, I mentally agreed with Susan's nasty word choice.

Moving quicker than me, Susan made it to the front door, unlocked it, and threw it open. "Chief Briggs. There was no need for dispatch to wake you up in the middle of the night. I have this well under control."

As the large man entered, he cast Susan a dismissive glance and headed my way. "You claim the poachers were in your store this evening, Ms. Page?"

Watson growled again at his approach, a little

more threat in the sound than the one he offered Susan.

I tightened my grip on his bandanna.

To my surprise, the chief didn't make any comment about impounding Watson. Nor did he sneer when he spoke to me. The two of us had only had a couple of interactions, but whereas Susan disdained me, seemed to relish in making my temperature rise, it was clear that Chief Briggs hated the very air I breathed, though I wasn't entirely sure what I'd ever done to earn that—outside of solving more murders in the past year than his police force.

I took just a second to make sure my tone matched the professionalism I heard in his. "Yes. They were talking about it. Referenced both the bighorn sheep and Leo and Watson's interruption— though of course they weren't named by name."

"Seems like a coincidence, doesn't it? You just happened to be present during that incident, and the two poachers show up at your bookshop two nights later?" A little of his professionalism cracked, letting some of his clear dislike seep through. "In my experience, poachers and book thieves are rarely the same individuals."

I should've called Branson. No matter if things were complicated between us personally, no matter that I was never entirely sure if he was going to be supportive or belittling, he never offered the contempt that Briggs and Green often did.

It was too late for that.

"From what I gathered, they came here planning to get marijuana plants or the supplies that were used in the grow house. It was my impression they'd hoped there were some left or that they'd not been discovered. I don't know. They mentioned Sid by name, but maybe they weren't clear on how long he's been dead." I managed to not sound the least bit irritated, and I considered that a win.

Chief Briggs balked, and for the first time in any of our interactions, he sounded interested. "Sid? Now there's a blast from the past." From his expression, it looked like the thought of the man left Briggs with a sour taste. Good to know I wasn't the only one who could cause that expression. "I'd hoped to never hear that man's name again."

At least he wasn't accusing me of lying or making it up. Though it was probably pointless after all the time that had passed, I figured I might as well push my luck and see if he'd believe me a second time. "The two of them also talked about Eddie and the Green Munchies. One of them wanted to head there to see if they could get... some produce, I believe, is how he termed it. The other didn't think that was a good idea, but... if they did, maybe you could catch them."

Another balk. "Eddie..." He took a step forward, causing Watson to growl again, but Chief Briggs didn't seem to notice. His eyes narrowed, and though he sounded skeptical, it seemed more out of disbelief than accusation. "You think these two men knew Sid and Eddie?"

"I didn't exactly have a conversation with them, Chief Briggs, but that's how it sounded. Or at least knew of them." As I spoke, the exact nature of what the larger man had said came back to me. I'd been so distracted by the mere mention of their names that I hadn't caught the implication. "I got the impression that he believed the same person killed Sid and Eddie, but... we all know who poisoned Sid. She didn't kill Eddie. *He* was shot, and that was never her style."

I hadn't really meant to say my thoughts out loud, and I braced myself for some new bit of scorn from Briggs for insinuating that I understood anything at all. To my surprise, there was no condescension as he spoke. "That is bizarre."

Susan must've felt the same surprise as I did. She looked at him in wonder. Not for the first time, I felt

a little bit of sympathy for her. Briggs barely treated
her with more respect than he did me, and she had to
work with him day after day. After a second, she
looked my way and attempted to join in. "You said
you got their names, didn't you, Fred?"

"Good grief, Green, I'm trying to think... Why
don't you..." Chief Briggs's snarl toward Susan broke
off, and he whipped toward me. "You got their
names?" His voice rose. "Holy Lord, woman, why
didn't you lead with that?"

I gripped Watson's bandanna tighter for good
measure as I reminded myself, at that moment, the
most important thing was catching Leo's poachers
and making sure the two men wouldn't come back
here. "There was a big guy named Max, huge, actually. And then another one named Jim—I didn't get
to see him. And one of them, Max, I think, referenced them being brothers."

Chief Briggs straightened and looked a little scary.
"Max and Jim." His low rumble of words seemed more
like he was talking to himself than either of us. "I was
right, most definitely a blast from the past." He met my
gaze, and once more, I was caught off guard by his
return to professionalism. "Good job, Ms. Page. It
makes sense now. Haven't heard hide nor hair of those

two idiots in a long, long time. I'd hoped they'd flung themselves off a cliff by now." He lifted his walkie-talkie to his lips and gave a directive for dispatch to contact Sergeant Wexler to head to the Green Munchies.

Once more, Susan looked as shocked as I felt. "Sir, if you need someone to—"

He cut her off with a glower and looked back at me. "I trust I can count on your discretion, at least for a couple of hours, before you call in your Scooby Gang and give them all the details?"

As I'd observed Chief Briggs, another part of my awareness was trying to fit the puzzle pieces together. "I still don't understand why they think the same person killed Sid and Eddie. It doesn't make any—"

"Max and Jim are two of the dumbest human pieces of—" He shook his head as if catching himself, and then glared again. "For the billionth time, Ms. Page, leave the murders to the cops. You'll only embarrass yourself." As if noticing Watson was there for the first time, Chief Briggs sneered down at him before turning and snapping his fingers at Susan. "*Clearly* things are under control here, *Officer* Green. Please go pretend to do something useful and not waste the taxpayers' money on your salary." He stormed away into the night, leaving the front door open behind him.

A glance at Susan revealed her cheeks were red with fury and maybe embarrassment.

I couldn't help myself. "Susan, don't let him—"

"Don't—" She swiped angrily in my direction but didn't look at me. She too left the Cozy Corgi.

FIVE

I gave up pretending to sleep a little after 4:00 a.m.

Watson, woken midsnore, glared through accusing eyes the second my foot hit the floorboard. Despite his grumpy feelings about being woken up, he popped out of bed and debated which of his stuffed animal bedfellows to bring. He snagged the yellow duck, made it a couple of feet, then rushed back and traded it for the fuzzy lion, before giving me an impatient chuff in his demand for breakfast.

"You're ridiculous." I ruffled his fur before heading to the kitchen.

I fried bacon and brewed a pot of coffee. For a moment, I considered taking it all to the front porch and letting my mind wander there as I stared into the dark forest that surrounded my little cabin. That notion scattered the second I opened the front door. Thick dark clouds covered the sky, obliterating the moon and stars, and there was the bite of snow in the air. Instead I settled in at the seafoam-green kitchen table. The coffeepot was in reach that way anyway. After a couple of slices of bacon, Watson plodded away, and within a few moments, his soft snores drifted back into the kitchen.

A million different scenarios of *what-ifs* played through my mind, just like they had when I'd lain in bed, staring at the ceiling. Somehow, with crispy bacon and hot coffee, they were a little less terrifying, but didn't fully evaporate either.

If Watson had barked or growled any louder than he had... If I'd sneezed as his fur wafted up to tickle my nose... If I'd gasped... If the larger man had looked to his right instead of his left...

Maybe the results would be the same. Maybe we would've startled each other, and they'd have run off. But from the sound of his voice—from *Max's* voice, I was never going to forget his name—I had a feeling he wasn't the type to turn and run. His brother Jim, maybe.

I didn't think they'd be back. Couldn't come up with a reason why they would. They hadn't found what they were looking for. Surely they had enough proof that all of Sid's pot plants and drug parapher-nalia had been discarded.

By the third cup of coffee, my mind traveled other bunny trails. For whatever reason, clearly Max had thought Sid's and Eddie's deaths were connected, and that if he and his brother tried to do anything at the pot shop in Lyons, they would meet the same fate.

It didn't make any sense. I knew who'd killed Sid, and she was in prison. As far as Eddie, I never met the person who killed him, but I'd seen the reports. His murder had been solved as well. And it most definitely had not been connected to Sid.

Unless I was wrong.

I stared at the yellow-and-green tie-dyed curtains covered in pink flamingos that hung over the window above the kitchen sink. The blurry, swirly pattern seemed to fit my frame of mind, despite the injection of caffeine. I was thinking crazy; I had to be. I wasn't wrong with what I knew.

"I was *there*. Well, I wasn't actually present when Sid was killed, but I was the one who heard the confession from his killer." I met the gaze of one of the pink flamingos.

It didn't respond.

"Maybe I'm being silly even considering what Max said. Clearly the two of them didn't know what they were doing. They were wrong about what they'd find in the Cozy Corgi, after all."

None of the flamboyant flock of flamingos said anything. "Who knows? Maybe I didn't even hear their conversation correctly. I was rather in a panic, and my heart was beating loud enough to wake the dead. In fact—" I suddenly realized I was talking to the flamingos on my curtains. It was one thing to talk things over with Watson; it was another to bounce ideas off flamingos, especially when those flamingos were nothing more than tacky material picked out by my stepfather. I stood up. "Well, if that's not a sign that I need to talk to a living person, I don't know what is. If you'll excuse me, I'm going to—" For crying out loud. I was *still* talking to the ridiculous flamingos.

I waved them off and didn't bother filling them in on my plans. Katie and Nick would've been at the bakery for a while already by that time. I'd go there. Have a second breakfast, more caffeine, and talk things over with the two of them. Maybe I'd help them prepare for the day. Although with my baking skills I'd probably only slow them down.

It was a little after five by the time Watson and I

hopped into my Mini Cooper and headed into town. If anything, the clouds had gotten heavier in the past hour; snow was definitely in the forecast. And though sunrise was less than three hours away, the morning was as dark as midnight.

As I came to the intersection of highways 36 and 34, I saw a figure walking her dog under the street-lamp across the way. She was just on the other side of what was commonly known as *Sheep Island*. In a decorative portion of the intersection, a large bronze bighorn ram stood proudly at the top of a rock outcropping, and below him, surrounded by land-scaped flowers and shrubbery was a bronze mother ewe and their little lamb.

Though Athena was bundled up against the cold, she was easily recognizable. I pulled the Mini Cooper into the nearby parking lot of a doughnut shop, snapped on Watson's leash, and caught up with Athena Rose within half a block.

Her white teacup poodle, Pearl, noticed us first and gave a happy yip.

Watson answered with one of his own and scur-ried to meet her. I wasn't sure if he would put it quite so formally, but the two most definitely had a crush on each other.

Athena's eyes narrowed and then widened in

pleased surprise. "Well, Winifred Page, what in tarnation are you doing out at this ungodly hour?"

"I can ask the same of you." I gave her a firm hug, and when she pulled back, I noticed a tightness in her smile and strain over her dark face. "Are you okay?"

She lifted a gloved hand to her cheek. "Apparently I don't look it."

I couldn't help but laugh. "Athena, it's *five* in the morning, and you look more glamorous walking your dog than I would if I'd had a team of stylists working on me for hours." There was only one woman I knew who would have her face fully painted, false eyelashes attached, and look ready to step onto the cover of *Vogue* at that hour in the morning.

She laughed along, but the sound didn't quite ring true. "I appreciate you saying that."

I noticed she didn't disagree with the sentiment. She was kind, but she was honest.

She bent and patted Watson. "Hello there, cute stuff. I was just thinking Pearl and I needed to come visit you soon."

Watson gave a quick lick to her gloved hand but refocused on nuzzling Pearl.

"I just saw Pearl's cute pink boots. She's almost as stylish as you."

"*Almost*, but she opted not to wear her tiara this morning." Athena straightened, and a little twinkle returned to her eyes. "I noticed from across the street that Watson actually dressed up last night. Sorry I didn't come over and say hello, but I was tired. I just came down long enough to give Paulie a break. I didn't even bring Pearl with me."

"He wore a bandanna. I don't know if that qualifies as a costume or not. The only reason he wore it was because Leo managed to get it on him." I reached for Athena's arm and gave it a gentle squeeze. "What's going on?"

She waved me off and started walking. I fell into step beside her, the two dogs trailing a few feet behind. "It's Odessa."

Apparently she was going to tell me after all. It took me half a second to remember who Odessa was. "Your granddaughter, the one who sings on Broadway?"

She nodded. "Yes. She's changing. Hardening somehow. I know it's a rough life. The expectations from producers and fellow actors and all the critics reviewing everything she does. Hard for any woman, but doubly so for a woman of color, especially one as beautiful as she is." Athena went silent for several steps, then shook her head. "She's not sounding like herself when I talk to her."

I wasn't sure how to respond. "You think maybe you might need to go visit?"

She smiled at me but didn't pause in her pace. "That was my first inclination, yes. But it's hard to know which mistakes to let you young ones make and when to try to rescue."

I doubted Odessa and I were anywhere near the same age, but I didn't make a comment about that. "If you're worried, maybe it would help you to see her."

Another smile, and this time Athena paused. "You're a darling, Fred, but it's clear you don't have grandchildren." She chuckled. "Obviously. But the point remains. Part of the parental role is trying to figure out when to stay away." She blinked rapidly, those long lashes fluttering, maybe even helping to drive away the tears. She shook her head, and her voice took on its more typical firm quality. "And you? You're not the type to go joyriding in the wee hours of the morning."

"No, not hardly." For a moment I considered turning things back to Odessa, wanting to make sure that I was a good friend, but decided that it seemed Athena was ready to move on.

I filled her in on the events of the night before, her sharp eyes grew shrewd during the retelling, after I spent several moments convincing her I was truly all right. "I can't say that Sid's passing was too big of a loss for this world, but the way he died seemed clear enough. And I have no question that we have the full story on that one. It made sense and went with the pattern. And I agree with you, I don't see how his death would be connected to that poor boy in Lyons." She paused again, considering. "Although they were both doing illegal drug trafficking. It sounds like it was rather on the small scale, but... that can't be discounted."

"But that had nothing to do with why Sid died."

"True." Athena started walking again, and we were getting close to the intersection once more where we'd started. "I'm inclined to think your other theory is correct. Those two hooligans that broke into your shop last night don't sound like the sharpest tools in the shed. I can't imagine they'd return."

And that brought us to the notion I'd had the moment I'd seen Athena walking under the streetlight. "I'm sure you're right, but..."

Shrewd indeed, when she turned narrow eyes to me once more, the streetlamp caught the playful glint. "You'd like me to use my resources at the paper to do some digging?"

Athena was the obituary writer at the *Chipmunk Chronicles*, and I figured there might be some answers in the archives there somewhere or through databases we couldn't access. "If you have time, either about Eddie or Sid. Maybe even Max and Jim. I know we don't have a last name, but I bet between you searching at the *Chipmunk* and me getting the Scooby Gang on it, we might find something."

"I'm not fond of Chief Briggs, but him labeling Katie, Leo, Paulie, and you the Scooby Gang was one of his more brilliant and apt moments." She chuckled. Though there was no traffic, we both paused at one of the green spaces, *Sheep Island,* between the stoplights and waited for the walk sign. "Honestly, it sounds like just the distraction I need. Count me in."

Watson growled and suddenly pulled at his leash.

I looked back at him. "What in the world, Watson?"

"Pearl! Stop that." Athena turned as well and started to scoop the little growling poodle into her arms. Before she did, she glanced to the side, gasped, and straightened with a jolt.

I followed to where she and the dogs were looking. I didn't notice it at first. In the dark of the night and the shadow cast by the large bronze ram and the jutting cropping of rock, it looked like nothing more than a mound of earth at the base of the statue of the mother and baby. Until I noticed a sliver of light illuminate a pale hand splayed palm up.

Now that I had seen it, despite the shadows, the picture became clear. I followed up the arm, which led to a large body equally splayed out over the flowers. There were drag marks through the plants that led to massive work boots. One of the broad shoulders lay at an angle, resting against the base of the rock with the head tilted back on another jut of stone like it was a pillow. The man's eyes were closed as if in sleep. But the bullet hole between his brows stripped away any illusion of dreams or pillows.

Beside me, Athena muttered a soft prayer and a curse.

Almost on instinct, I stepped forward, trying to get a better look.

Athena grabbed my wrist and brought me to a pause. Even so, she leaned forward as well. "Who is it?" Her voice didn't shake or even have a hint of panic. "I don't recognize him. A tourist?"

I started to say that I didn't know who he was either, but then there was something familiar about

him. Shifting slightly, I got a different angle and realized I did indeed know him. The flattened nose that
had clearly been broken multiple times. The
work boots.

Though he was clearly no longer a threat, at the
recognition, remembered fear from a few hours
before coursed through me. When I spoke, I could
hear the tremble in my words. "Max. That's Max."

"Who is—" Before she finished, Athena let out
an understanding sigh. "Oh."

"Yeah." The two of us stared, and when Watson
got close enough to nudge his nose on the man's boot,
I realized my grip had gone slack on his leash and I
pulled him back. "Watson, no."

He obeyed and trotted back to me. As he did,
Pearl stopped pulling on her leash and settled in
beside him.

I glanced around, looking for Jim—not that I
would recognize the other intruder, but I figured if
there was another body, it would be self-explanatory.
I didn't see one. Finally, I turned to Athena. "Would
you mind calling the police this time? Technically
you saw it first. That way it won't increase the body
count that I keep stumbling over."

Katie and the Pacheco twins greeted Watson and me as we walked into the Cozy Corgi. It was still early enough that we had half an hour before opening.

Watson, who'd been in a sullen, irritated mood after an exorbitant amount of chaotic time with the police, bounced at the sight of Ben, gave a happy bark, and rushed toward one of his favorite humans. In response, Ben knelt, tucked a strand of shoulder-length black hair behind his ears, and greeted Watson with open arms. "Hi, my friend." He pressed a kiss to Watson's nose and kept stroking him as he smiled up at me, his tone warm and little more than a whisper. "Good to see you too."

Beside him, his even quieter twin brother, Nick, nodded and gave a wave.

Katie mimicked Watson and hurried my way, throwing her arms around me. "Are you okay?" She squeezed so tight I couldn't answer, and then let go only to grip my arms just as firm. She glared up into my face, her voice transitioning from worried to angry. "Obviously you're okay. Why in the world did you not call me last night?"

"Last night?" I blinked, that wasn't what I'd expected. "I figured you'd heard about what Athena and I found this morning."

She gave me a shake. "I did! I *also* heard that the body belonged to some horrid man who broke in here last night, and that he was the poacher who killed the sheep when we were with Leo the night before!" Another shake. "And again, why didn't you call me? He must've been here when I left you. You could've been—"

"I'm okay." Warmed by her concern, I laughed and twisted free. "Honestly, the only physical harm I've experienced is the bruising that's going to occur on my arms from your fingers digging in."

Her cheeks blushed, and she tilted her chin in the air. "Serves you right."

"And I'm sorry I didn't call. I knew you'd be back in here in the blink of an eye, and you needed your sleep. Besides, there was nothing you could do. It was over. I was on my way in here this morning to talk things over with you and Nick when I saw

Athena walking and we found the body of one of the intruders." I glanced over Katie's shoulder where Ben was still lavishing Watson with attention. "Why are you here so early?"

"I came in with Nick." He lifted one hand and made a circle gesture encompassing the shop. "I thought we agreed that we would decorate after Halloween was over."

Watson head-butted his knee, demanding both Ben's hands be on him.

Ben chuckled and obliged.

I glanced at the Cozy Corgi, surprised I hadn't noticed the change despite getting accosted the second I walked in. "Ben, wow! How in the world did you do so much? You completely transformed the place."

There was the typical fall and Thanksgiving décor all over the shop—assortments of pumpkins and dried gourds and large stalks of corn, revealing multicolored kernels within their husks, arranged artfully at the ends of shelves. Colorful turkey cutouts placed here and there. Yellow, orange, and brown streamers draped artfully over the counter in the center of the shop. And amid all of that, were posters and framed art depicting the Ute deities of Wolf, who was the creator, and Coyote, his younger trickster brother. There were illustrations and descriptions of both the sun and bear dances and a large beaded circle depicting the Ute symbol. A couple of mannequin busts were on stands—one displaying fringed buckskin decorated with deer teeth and the other wearing jewelry of seeds and juniper berries and turquoise with bear claws below a headdress of feathers and more beadwork.

Katie and I had been midpreparation with our plans for decorating for Thanksgiving when we wondered how that would make Ben and Nick feel, especially considering some of the discrimination they'd experienced as Native Americans from select people in town. The twins instantly volunteered to bring in some items they'd collected over the years.

I was blown away. "Ben, Nick, this... is amazing. Absolutely beautiful. Thank you for—"

"Later! Good grief!" Katie went shrill, which was very atypical of her. "Are you sure you're okay?"

"Yes! I'm fine. Watson and I both are. I was scared more than anything." I walked around her and headed past the twins and Watson to shove my purse under the counter. "I was coming in to talk to you about some of the things I overheard the intruders say last night, but then, as you heard, we found one of their bodies."

"At the sheep statues." Nick spoke, but it wasn't a question.

I answered anyway. "Yes." I considered the time. "Shouldn't you be getting to school? We don't want to give them any reason to cause you more problems."

He grinned. "I'll be fine as long as I leave in the next ten minutes."

Katie joined me at the counter, and when she spoke, she sounded more like herself. "It didn't hit me until right now, hearing Nick say that. The poacher who killed the bighorn sheep was found dead at the statue of the *bighorn sheep*?"

I opened my mouth to reply and halted. "Yeah... I... hadn't thought of that, either."

"It sounds like you've been a little busy." Ben gave me another smile but turned his attention back to Watson. "Both of you."

"That's true, we have, but..." I refocused on Katie. "That's interesting. Although, I'm not entirely sure I got the impression, from what the brothers were saying..." I rushed to clarify at Katie's puzzled expression. "The intruders were brothers—Max and Jim. Max is the dead one, but like I was saying, I got the impression that Jim was the one who killed the sheep. At least Max was blaming him for leaving it behind and not taking care of Leo and Watson."

Katie's eyes went wide as she gripped the counter. "Taking care of Leo and Watson?"

I shrugged. "I don't know if that's too big a shock. I mean, we were all thinking it. Running into the woods toward a person who'd just killed an animal. We heard the gunshot."

"I know…" She shivered. "But still, it was just confirmed."

The front door of the bookstore was flung open —apparently I'd forgotten to lock it when I entered.

"Fred!" My tiny mother practically flew across the floor, rushed around the counter, and like Katie only a few minutes before, threw her arms around me. "You're okay! I've been calling and calling. When you didn't answer—"

"I told you she was fine, dear. Fred can handle herself. Plus, none of the gossip said she was hurt." My stepfather, Barry, entered the Cozy Corgi and shut the door behind him.

Watson let out another happy yip, gave another hop, and rushed toward Barry, another of his favorite people. If only Leo would enter, he could have his perfect trifecta. He made it halfway to Barry before skidding to a halt and looking back at Ben, clearly torn. He whimpered and trembled.

Laughing, Barry closed the distance, put one hand on his head and used his other to motion toward Ben. "Join us before Watson has a heart attack. He's been through too much the way it is."

Ben had already been on his way, and Watson was lost to pure heaven. The three of them managed to stir up an impressive cloud of dog hair in the process.

Mom spoke again, and for the second time that morning, I got scolded. "Why didn't you answer? I was worried sick all the way here."

"I didn't know you called. I guess I shoved my cell in my purse in all the chaos and never got it back out. I'm sorry." I shook my head, laughing, and pointed between her and Katie. "You know, you two have a funny way of showing that you love me. I survived a break-in last night and discovered a body this morning, and *I'm* the one getting in trouble."

"You are just like your father." Mom *tsked* and shook her head. "A magnet for danger." She paused to glare at my chest. "Are you wearing your necklace?"

I pulled it out and held up between us the sky-blue crystal of celestine Mom had made me a few months before. "You asked me to always wear it, so I do."

"Good, now take it off." She held out her hand.

Knowing better than to question, I did as she asked.

Her fingers barely closed around it before she started toward the door. "I'm going over to Chakras. I have a key. Although Verona and Zelda should be there any minute. Celestine is good for calming, balance, and remembering dreams, but you need something stronger, clearly. I should have insisted on it from the beginning. I'll be right back."

Barry grinned after her as she hurried out of the shop and then smiled over at me from where he and Ben still knelt on either side of Watson. "Seems like you're doing just fine with the celestine to me, but who knows? Maybe you'll do even better with something else." His watery blue eyes warmed as he inspected me. "Sure you're okay, darling?"

"I am. Just shaken, but apparently not enough, judging from everyone's reactions." Truth be told, though it probably shouldn't be thought, I was less shaken than I'd been all through the night. I hadn't really thought that the intruders would come back, but the one who'd scared me was now no longer a threat. I wouldn't go so far as to say I was glad he was dead, but of all the dead bodies I'd discovered, his was the first one that had brought a sense of relief. "What I really need, Katie, is a dirty chai and as many pastries as you can fit on a platter." I grinned at her. "In the last twelve hours, I've had two rather unpleasant interactions with both Susan Green and Chief Briggs. Caffeine and sugary carbs won't fix it, but they'll sure help."

"No Branson?" Katie cocked an eyebrow.

I shook my head. Maybe he'd called. His message might be waiting in the cell alongside my mother's.

When Nick left for school, the rest of us headed up to the bakery. We were seated around the table, sharing an assortment of Katie and Nick's creations and I'd only had my second sip of dirty chai when the first of the morning's customers came up the stairs in search of both nourishment and gossip.

It was going to be a morning. Actually, it was going to be a day. With most of the tourists gone from the Halloween festivities of the night before, there wouldn't be many books sold, but with the events of the night before and the morning, every last local and their dog would be in for the latest. And from the completely restocked pastry cases, it looked like Katie was more than prepared.

Before too long, with Ben manning the bookshop below and Katie filling bakery and coffee orders, Mom came up the steps followed by Verona and Zelda, my stepsisters. The three of them hurried to the table where Barry and I still sat and took the seats that Anna and Carl had just vacated.

"Here. The girls gave their input." Mom thrust my necklace back at me. It still had the larger sky-blue crystal in the center, but it was now bookended by a shiny black stone and a shimmering blue-green one that resembled the color of a peacock feather. "The black tourmaline was my idea. It repels lower harmful frequencies. The girls..." She grimaced. "Well, Verona, decided on the labradorite."

"It shields against psychic attacks and ill wishes." Verona tapped the peacock-hued crystal. "You never know."

Zelda crossed her arms, sounding somewhat putout. "I wanted rose quartz. There's no better defense against darkness than love. Plus I think the pink would have been a good addition to the necklace."

Mom gave a soothing pat to Zelda's shoulder. "I know dear. But Fred's been very clear about anything to do with love and relationships. This necklace is about protection." She fluttered her fingers at me. "Put it on."

I did, Barry lending a hand by holding my long auburn hair out of the way but accidentally getting it entangled in the dangling earrings of silver corgis. After all was put to rights, he dusted some croissant crumbs from his tie-dyed shirt and made Watson very happy from his place under the table.

Sure enough, the steady stream of customers didn't stop for five solid hours, transitioning from breakfast to midmorning snack, lunch, and beyond. Each one wanted details about the break-in and the discovery of Max's body. By the time all the pastries were devoured, Nick had returned from his half day at school and helped Katie start afresh. For the billionth time, I wondered how the two of us had managed the few months without the twins. They were godsends, both of them.

Things had started to slow down, and I was getting ready to head back to the bookshop when Leo, in his park ranger uniform, appeared at the top of the steps, his brown eyes panicked and searching the space before they landed on me.

Watson noticed Leo when he was halfway across the bakery and rushed toward him. For the first time I could remember, Leo merely dipped slightly, just enough to brush his fingertips down Watson's back, but didn't so much as pause.

More than anything else, that made my adrenaline kick in. I stood as he reached me. "What's wrong?"

"The police. They just—" He shook his head, a crease forming between his brows as he leveled his gaze on me. "Sorry, first things first. I shouldn't take for granted just because you're tough that you're okay." He gripped my arms as Katie had earlier, but his touch was gentle, and he didn't shake. "*Are* you okay?"

For whatever reason, the way he asked, or the tender care in his eyes, I felt some of my strength crumble. The feeling surprised me. As did the tears that threatened to burn right behind my eyes. Maybe I wasn't as unaffected as I thought. Feeling ridiculous, I blinked the emotion away. "I am. Thank you. Watson and I were safe last night too." I shrugged and forced a laugh. "Well... as you're aware, it was hardly my first time seeing a dead body."

"I know, but just because you've gone through it

a couple of times doesn't mean it doesn't take its toll." A smile played his lips. "I'm glad you're okay."

Katie appeared beside us. "Leo, are you all right?"

He grinned over at her. "I was just asking the same of Fred." He gave my arms a soft squeeze and let me go, and then his gaze turned hard and worried again as he glanced around. "Is there someplace we can talk in private? I know it's going to spread through the gossip chain like wildfire within the next half an hour, but I don't want it to come from me."

Katie groaned. "Something else happened?"

He nodded, then looked at me expectantly.

I considered. We could go to the storeroom, but it would be rather cramped, or the storage space underneath the bookshop, but after the events of the night before I didn't really want to be down there for any reason.

Katie came to the rescue and pointed through the bakery. "Let's go to the back of the kitchen. We'll be mostly out of view, and with the noise of the mixers, dishwashers and such, we won't be overheard. If Nick happens to hear something, he's not the type to spread it around."

"Good enough." Leo gave a nod, and he and I followed Katie.

I paused at the edge of the bakery and knelt toward Watson, who was staring at Leo with hurt in his eyes. "Sorry, buddy, I need you to stay here for a little bit." Though I didn't do a perfect job of keeping him out of the kitchen portion of the bakery, I at least needed to do so when we had a room full of customers. Although, since they were all locals, they had no illusions about Watson not being the king of the Cozy Corgi—the bookshop *and* the bakery.

Leo knelt beside me, finally taking Watson's face in his hands and rubbing his cheeks with his thumbs. "Sorry, little man. I wasn't trying to ignore you."

Watson whimpered and his knob of a tail wagged, causing his whole fuzzy butt to shimmy in happiness.

Despite whatever was going on, Leo's affection was clear in his patient tone. "I'll come down and see you in a bit, but for now, go be with Ben."

Watson's little brows rose.

"Good idea." I patted Leo's arm and then Watson's head before pointing toward the stairs. "Ben, Watson. Go to Ben."

I nearly laughed at the war that clearly waged behind Watson's honey-brown eyes, the pull of desire between two of his dear loves. Finally, once Leo pulled his hands away, Watson took a few steps backward, then with a huff, whirled and took off through the bakery and down the steps.

Leo chuckled, but by the time he stood, his expression was serious again.

We joined Katie, who was already in the back of the kitchen with her hands on her hips. "What happened? More poaching?"

"No." Leo shook his head, and though his gaze darted between Katie and me, it focused longer on me. "The police just arrested Nadiya for that man's murder. She didn't do it. The police are adamant about it, and as ever, Branson and the chief won't listen to me."

A check through the voicemails revealed that Branson hadn't called or texted. Apparently he'd been busy. I didn't need further explanation from Leo, and I sighed. "You want me to look into it."

He started to nod, then paused. "Only if it's not going to upset you or put you at risk. I know you've got to be shaken after last night. And from what I've heard, there were two intruders, so there's still one out there."

Katie answered for me. "Of course she'll look into it, and it's not like she won't have you and me helping her." She grinned my way. "Plus, I think I just saw a delivery of a magically protective necklace."

I didn't have to consider. Leo was clearly upset. There was nothing he or Katie could request that I wouldn't do. Besides, at this point, even I couldn't pretend that it took much of a motive for me to try to solve a murder. "Of course I will, you know that."

Katie nodded in approval, then turned a questioning gaze on Leo. "Are you sure Nadiya *didn't* have anything to do with it? He was a poacher after all, and she seemed pretty emphatic last night about what she thought should happen to poachers."

While I didn't necessarily disagree with her, I was a little surprised Katie would verbalize the thought. Though I tried, I couldn't read if it was a genuine concern or if Katie had decided she didn't quite care for Nadiya Hameed.

Leo also surprised me with his resigned sigh. "I admit, it looks bad. Nadiya is... passionate in her animal advocacy, and if she'd caught him in the act of killing an animal"—he grimaced—"well... maybe, but that wasn't the case here. She insists she didn't do it. I believe her. She's become a good friend, and she is one of the best park rangers I've ever seen, one we've needed for a long time." He held my gaze once more. "I hate to ask it of you, but—"

"Stop it. Anything for you, or you." I grinned to Katie. "There's no request that's too big between us. Besides, we all know I like solving murders just as much as settling down with a good book."

"I wouldn't go that far." Katie winked.

Though I didn't say so, I kinda thought I enjoyed solving a murder even more.

SEVEN

Leo and Katie came to my cabin after closing the Cozy Corgi. By late afternoon, the ominous clouds that had been threatening all day let loose, and within an hour Estes Park was transformed into a winter wonderland. Though the snowstorm slowed, there didn't appear to be any sign of it stopping.

Katie and Leo made tomato soup while I worked on grilled cheeses, and then we spent the next couple of hours going back and forth between Leo filling us in about Nadiya and attempting to uncover anything we could about Max and Jim.

Katie and I curled up together on the couch, poring over our laptops while Leo took a similar position by the roaring fire, searching his computer while never ceasing to stroke Watson.

On the one hand, between the friendship and the fire, it was a pleasant evening with the beautiful snow drifting down on the other side of the windows. On the other, it was frustrating. We couldn't find anything about the poachers. Nothing. There'd still not been a solitary word from Branson, and I wasn't about to call and ask for details anymore.

Even getting Leo's perspective on Nadiya wasn't overly helpful. He painted a picture of a passionate and devoted park ranger, one who tirelessly wrote to political leaders requesting stricter animal protection laws and was active in animal-rights marches.

By the time they left, the snow was a couple of inches thick, and it didn't feel like we were any closer to figuring out who the poachers were, if there was any possible connection to the Green Munchies in Lyons, or helping Nadiya.

Deciding that my brain had reached its fill between the stress of the night before, the lack of sleep, and the nonstop events of the day, I slipped into my flannel nightgown, picked up the newest Dean Koontz novel I'd started right before Halloween, and settled into the armchair in front of the fire with Watson at my feet. I was willing to bet I'd make it a total of four pages before falling asleep. Maybe by the light of a new day, with a rested brain and body, I'd have an idea of where to begin.

I made it two and a half pages before a growl

rumbled from Watson and he trotted toward the front door. An arrow of fear shot through me, my first notion being that Max's brother had come to get his revenge. I shoved that aside. It was a ridiculous thought born of exhaustion. Jim didn't know I'd been hiding in the mystery room while he and his brother discussed poaching and stole the contents of the cash register. And as far as revenge, I wasn't the one who'd killed Max.

Refusing to give in to fear, I set the book aside, stood, and nearly caught up with Watson by the time a knock sounded. Even then, despite myself, my adrenaline spiked. Again, ridiculous. If the ludicrous happened and Jim was at the door, he would hardly knock. He'd just kick it in. Although from what I'd overheard, that sounded more like his brother's style.

I peered through the peephole and was met with darkness. For a second I thought whoever was there was covering the peephole with their hand, but then I realized I'd not turned on the front porch light. Leaning over I did so and looked back once more.

Relief washed over me at the sight of Branson Wexler's handsome face, but it was quickly followed by a different sort of anxiety.

For a couple of seconds, I considered not answering, pretending not to be home. I was exhausted and on edge. I'd either say something to him I'd regret or allow myself to feel things for him I had no business feeling.

Another knock.

Watson growled.

"Fred?" Branson's voice was muffled. "If you wanted to pretend you weren't home, you shouldn't have turned on the porch light."

"I might have installed one of those motion sensitive ones." I couldn't help myself.

"My bad, that must be what it is." His warm chuckle issued through the door. "I'll come back when you're home."

Joining in his laughter, I released locks and opened the door.

He smiled at me and glanced down when Watson growled again. "For the billionth time, little man, your mom is safe with me. Always."

Watson gave a final rumble, a chuff, and then turned around and sauntered back toward the fire as if tossing his front paws in the air in surrender.

Branson focused on me once more as he motioned through the door. "May I come in? That is, if you're sure that you're home."

I rolled my eyes and stood back, giving him room. "Come on in."

He started to, then paused, stamped the snow from his boots onto the welcome mat, dusted off his jacket, and then entered. By the time I turned around from locking the door, he'd removed his jacket and scarf. He wasn't in uniform, but wearing dark-wash jeans and a deep green sweater that brought out the brighter hue in his eyes.

He started to say something, sniffed, and glanced toward the kitchen. "Tomato soup and grilled cheese?"

I nodded. "You know me, it's snowing outside, so I've got to have my tomato soup and grilled cheese."

He hesitated, looking nervous, which was always a strange expression on his strong face. "Got any leftovers?"

A sudden pang of loss settled over me, and the year folded in on itself to a night so similar to this one. The first time Branson had been in my home we'd shared an identical meal.

I knew I should tell him no, see why he had come, and then send him on his way. Maybe it was the exhaustion, or feeling sentimental due to the extreme swing of emotions the past day had brought. Whatever it was, I sighed and headed into the kitchen. "I'll warm up the soup and make some fresh grilled cheeses."

"You don't have to go to any trouble."

There was my out, if I needed one. I didn't take it. "And deprive Watson of yet another unhealthy snack? I wouldn't be that cruel." I'd already had two grilled cheese sandwiches with Katie and Leo. The last thing I needed was another one. Perhaps that wasn't true, as I suddenly needed one desperately.

I retrieved the pot of soup out of the fridge and swiped up the frying pan that had been air-drying on the towel by the sink.

Branson stood by the stove. "May I help you with anything?"

The question caused another ache, and I turned to look at him, partially frozen in place. I wasn't sure if those had been his exact words or not the year before, but the sentiment had been the same, and that had caused my heart to skip a beat, even more than his movie-star good looks. My ex-husband had been the kind to not do so much as lift a finger, only demand and criticize. He hadn't started out that way, but after years of marriage, I realized I had been the proverbial toad in the pot, never noticing just how hot the water had become.

Branson's brows knitted. "Sorry, did I say something wrong?"

"No." Mentally I gave myself shake. "Sorry. I

appreciate the offer. It's been a long day, more than a long day. I'm just tired and..." I blinked, feeling a little exposed, but despite how things had ended between us, what Branson said to Watson had been true. I was always safe with him. "I'm a little overly emotional."

For the billionth time, he proved he was not my ex-husband. "Anyone would be after the time you've had. Hiding during a robbery last night and then finding yet another body this morning."

"Heard about that, did you?" The moment needed lightening. "Funny, I thought I'd managed to keep it a secret." I found my movement once again and put the frying pan on the stovetop. At the sound, Watson rushed into the kitchen and took sentinel by the stove, waiting for any morsel to accidentally fall onto the floor.

"Well..." Branson winked. "As secrets go in Estes, it was a pretty well-kept one. Luckily, I'm a policeman, so I have the inside scoop. That and the whole town might be talking about it."

I gave a pretend wince. "Oh, right. There was that." I motioned toward the table. "Thanks for the offer, but go ahead and have a seat. Grilled cheeses are a one-man job." I didn't give him a chance to respond before I kept going. "Did you just get back into town?" I nearly clarified that I was referencing the night of the break-in, since he'd clearly been in town at some point as he'd refused to listen to Leo's concerns.

Branson hadn't moved from his spot beside the stove and tilted his head quizzically at me. "No. I wasn't out of town."

I'd started to head toward the refrigerator to get the cheese that I'd forgotten when I retrieved the pot of soup, but I froze, looking back at him. "You weren't? You were in Estes last night and early this morning?"

"Yeah, why?" His confused expression softened, and his shoulders slumped. "Oh, because I didn't come to the Cozy Corgi last night or to the crime scene this morning."

Branson had been in town.

Hurt trickled in, closely followed by anger. Anger at myself for feeling hurt. Branson often disappeared for a day or two on overnight trips in his role as sergeant, and I'd just assumed that was where he'd been. It was the only reason he ever missed an occasion when I called the police. I had no right to be hurt by the fact that he didn't come this time. None at all.

"Fred, I'm sorry..." He reached for me.

"No." I held up a hand, but in what I hoped wasn't an unkind way. "You have no reason to be sorry. You're only respecting my wishes. So... thank you." Strangely, saying those words helped both alleviate the feeling of hurt and the guilt around it. Things were exactly how they should be. Except for Branson being in my kitchen and me making him a late-night snack.

He hesitated, then gave one of his bright smiles, though it seemed slightly forced, and finally crossed the kitchen and plopped down at the table. "You know, I honestly forgot I didn't tell you this. When the edict was passed down, I considered giving you advanced warning but then figured from what you said, you wouldn't want me to. As much as I went back and forth trying to decide, I think I truly forgot that I didn't tell you."

I tried to decipher that for the correct meaning and failed. Finally I just laughed. "*What?*"

"I guess that wasn't very clear, was it?" Branson gave a laugh of his own, then darkened somewhat. "My... superior has forbidden me from being part of any investigation where you are even slightly involved, or answering any calls you make." His gaze rose and locked on to mine. "I was here last night and this morning, but I wasn't allowed to take part or to help."

"Chief Briggs said to..." The surprise that had risen faded instantly, and I propped my hip against the oven door, the cheese slices still in my hands. "Of course he did." I thought back to his and Susan's interaction at the Cozy Corgi. "Was the opposite decree passed down to Susan?"

He nodded.

"Is that punishment for me or her?"

He winced a little. "Both. I believe."

Strangely, the knowledge infused a sense of kinship for Officer Green. Unsure how to respond, I decided not to, and turned back to the stove to start in on the grilled cheeses.

Watson began to whimper in anticipation as soon as the smell of melting butter filled the kitchen.

As I prepared Branson's and my sandwiches, I put mayonnaise on mine the way I liked it and left his plain. I paused with the mayonnaise-covered knife in midair, staring at the bread slices. I didn't have to ask him how he liked his grilled cheese. I already knew. And again that sense of loss.

It had been a mistake. I shouldn't have been making sandwiches for him, not when I was exhausted and emotional and on edge. Not when I was prone to only see the wonderful and charming parts of Branson, when I was tempted to overlook the other aspects. True, he'd never been as dismissive or commanding as my ex-husband, but he'd gotten close. And ultimately it didn't matter if those times had been because of commands he'd gotten from a superior or not. We'd crossed this bridge. It wasn't fair to me to be tempted to walk back across it just because of the moment we were in. Nor was it fair to him.

I'd make it fast.

After the sandwiches were sizzling on the frying pan, I returned things to business as I stirred the warming tomato soup. I made certain my voice was going to be neutral when I spoke, not cold, but not overly familiar either. "So, did you come here to just check in? Just make sure that I'm safe on your off-time so you're not breaking orders?"

"Yes, partly."

Partly. Despite my best effort I turned to him in surprise.

"That is most definitely the main reason I'm here." Branson's tone shifted to neutral as well. "We had several calls from Leo Lopez this afternoon, and I have no doubt he's requested for you to get involved in trying to clear Nadiya Hameed's name.

I thought I would come out here to circumvent that."

And there we were. I bristled. "Let me get this straight. You came here to check on me, which is appreciated. I'm fine. Thank you." I still attempted to keep a neutral tone, though I figured I wouldn't be able to pull it off. "But you're also here, not in uniform, on your off-time, and when you've been given explicit instructions to stay away from me as far as police business is concerned, to tell me to keep my nose out of it?"

He opened his mouth, and I saw a flash of anger behind his eyes, but then it was gone as he laughed. "I've made that mistake more than once, and it should have only taken me one time to realize it wasn't going to work."

"Does that mean you're not—" A faint burning scent reached my nose, and I paused to flip the sandwiches before looking back at him. "Does that mean you're not here to tell me to keep my nose out of it?"

"Would it do any good?" Though his eyes crinkled playfully, the humor didn't quite reach his voice.

"You know the answer to that."

"Yes, I do." He leaned back in the chair, stretching out his legs and accidentally bumping the sole of his boot against Watson's flank. "Sorry, little buddy."

Watson answered with a glare, shuffled closer to the oven, and looked up at me expectantly.

I tore off a corner of a fresh slice of bread and tossed it to him before looking over at Branson, probably giving him an identical expression to the one Watson had just given me.

He didn't need any more prompting. "I know you're going to look into Nadiya. Both because Leo will want you to and simply because you're Winifred Page—that's... what you do." He must've realized the exasperated sound in his tone as he raised both his hands in surrender. "And you do it well. Anyone who says otherwise is either an idiot or a liar. You're smart, capable, and insightful."

I took a moment to plate the sandwiches, ladle two bowls of tomato soup, and place them on the table. "But...?" I sat down across from him, and as was typical with Branson, I had the sensation I was both sitting down to a meal with a friend—someone who was extremely important to me—and yet sitting down with an adversary. "There's a *but* coming."

Proving the second sensation correct, Branson continued. "But... you'll be wasting your time on this one. There is no doubt that Nadiya is guilty. I know

Leo believes differently." He rolled his eyes. "Trust me, I've gotten more than an earful today. I know he means well. He's proven that over the countless, and I do mean *countless*, calls and complaints he's made about poaching in the park."

I'd started to take a bite of the grilled cheese but didn't. "And he was right, just like with Sid being involved in the poaching. Leo tried to tell you that Sid was part of it, but none of you would listen."

Again he offered the hands of surrender. "And I've admitted, and will admit again, that he was right and we were wrong. But in our defense, he had absolutely no shred of proof. None. Not until you came along with that owl feather."

I leaned across, and even as I did so, I wasn't sure why I was trying so desperately to convince him. "But that's just my point. It's always been my point. I can look into things in a different way than you can, without breaking any laws. You could never have found that feather without a search warrant—I could. If Leo believes Nadiya is innocent, then she is. And I'll help prove it. Maybe in ways that you're not able to. We both know I don't need your permission, and since you're not allowed to be talking to me about it anyway, this is all beside the point."

"It isn't beside the point." Branson matched my

position but leaned forward a little farther and placed a hand on my forearm. "There are no missing pieces to this, Fred. Nadiya is guilty. She did this." His gaze darkened, just for a flash. "And part of me, the man I am when I'm not in uniform, is glad that she did."

I flinched.

"I am. I admit it." His thumb made a solitary caress over my skin. "I have no doubt that you were in danger last night, none. This man, Max, was a threat to you. Chances are high you wouldn't have been in jeopardy from him again, but..." He shrugged. "Who knows? But now, thanks to Nadiya, that's no longer a possibility. And from everything that's known about Jim, you're not in danger from him either." He released my arm and sat back. "But when I'm in uniform, I have to admit that Nadiya took the law into her own hands in a very violent and deadly way."

I couldn't figure out how to answer that, overwhelmed by what he'd just admitted. I tore off a bit of my grilled cheese and handed it to Watson, partly to give myself a moment to think. Finally I looked back at Branson, deciding to just skip completely over the "he was glad Max was dead" part. "But what if Leo's right? He has been before, and he knows her, apparently very well. If he's convinced she's innocent, that she wouldn't kill someone, then I believe him. I've never gotten in the police's way before. I've never broken any laws. I won't this time either. But it's not going to hurt you or the police force if I... do my thing."

"It might hurt you."

"I thought you weren't going to tell me to keep my nose out of it."

Brandon flinched, but then he shrugged. "You might've noticed that Chief Briggs is fed up with your involvement. And he's not going to hurt you, obviously, but if you slip up, even a little, and do something outside the lines, he's going to bring the full weight of the law against you."

"And what does that say about him?"

He'd taken a bite of grilled cheese and chewed it before speaking. "You're the daughter of a detective, Fred. Don't pretend to be ignorant. Just because the chief doesn't want a civilian butting their nose into every murder that happens doesn't make him a bad man. Would your father have welcomed a layperson barging into his investigations?"

I started to argue the points but couldn't. So I didn't try. "That doesn't change the fact that you have—*may* have—an innocent woman in custody for murder. And from what Leo said, you're not letting anyone speak to her. No one can get her side."

"Just because Leo doesn't get a chance to talk to Nadiya doesn't mean squat." Branson thumped the tabletop with his forefinger and caused Watson to let out a startled yip below. "He's not her lawyer, he's not her husband, he's not family—he's nothing to her besides a coworker and a friend. He has no legal standing. I promise you that Nadiya is getting every right to which she is entitled. She'll have legal representation, the whole nine yards. Just because Leo doesn't get what *he* wants doesn't mean there's a conspiracy."

Even at the best of times, with his tone my rage would've boiled, but in my exhausted state, it took every single ounce of willpower to bite my tongue. Because somewhere in there, beneath that tone that sounded like my ex-husband, I knew he was right. In every single thing.

Branson cocked his head, and his volume lowered. "Sorry if I sounded harsh, but I need you to wake up."

I'd started to soften at the beginning of his apology and then had to grip the edge of the table to keep from losing my temper. I managed to speak through gritted teeth. "You need me to *wake up?*"

That time Branson started to speak, but I cut him off. "What you said is true. Leo doesn't have any legal right to see Nadiya or get her side of things. But you also have to admit that it would hardly be the first time someone in this town has been set up for murder, or that the police department has gotten the wrong person in a cell." It was my turn to punch the table with my finger, and Watson let out yet another yip, but I couldn't bring myself to comfort him. "You also have to admit, that if it wasn't for me sticking my nose into things where it didn't belong and refusing to butt out, some of those people would still be in jail. So why should I trust that that isn't true with Nadiya this time?"

Branson opened his mouth several times and closed it. Each time an array of emotions flickered over his face, shifting from anger to hurt to frustration to resignation. Finally, leaving the rest of his food uneaten, he stood. "This was a mistake on my part. I'm sorry. I should've listened to my chief. But..." When he met my gaze, though his eyes were hard, there was sorrow there. "I can't protect you anymore, Fred. While you're technically right, you haven't broken any laws, Chief Briggs is well within his right to expect you to let the police do their jobs." He turned and was nearly to the kitchen door before he looked back at me. "Here's my final overreach for you. Even though I shouldn't even give you these details, I hope that it will convince you to stay out of it. We found the murder weapon in the cab of Nadiya's truck."

"Maybe someone planted it. It's obvious that—"

He cut me off with a growl and a swipe of his hand. "She was *in* the truck at the time. Caught by the police in Lyons, not us. There was blood in the bed of the truck, which I'm sure will come back as a positive match for Max's. There were drag marks and mud in the bed well. And that's just a few of the details. I won't even get into Nadiya's past and what else she's done. Mainly because it would be breaking the law to tell you, but also because it's none of your business." His expression softened once more. "I hate that this is where we are. I hoped... I hope..." He shook his head. "I have always told you, you'll always be safe with me. But... I can't protect you anymore, not when you're too stubborn to let me. Being a detective's daughter won't protect you from the law."

He didn't wait for a reply, not that I would've been able to come up with one, before he retrieved his scarf and jacket and walked out of my house.

EIGHT

By late morning, the snow had started again, not in thick torrents as it had the day before, but in large fluffy flakes that drifted lazily outside the windows. During the summer, I had played the part of a crazy person by lighting the fire in the mystery room and having the windows open so it wouldn't get too hot. Now it was cold enough that both fireplaces in the Cozy Corgi were roaring, and I was snuggled on the sofa under the antique lamp in my favorite room, of course. Unfortunately, though I'd assumed the position, I held no new or well-loved book in my hands, but instead was searching away on the computer perched on my lap.

In frustration, I looked up from the screen. I'd been searching the internet for too long; maybe I needed a break. I peered into the main room, where Ben leaned against the front counter and scribbled in a notebook. Doubtlessly, he was mapping out plot points for a series of mystery novels he hoped to write that revolved around an incarnation of the Ute deity, Coyote. It was rare for him to turn to the notebook. Even in lulls between customers, Ben always found some chore to do—straightening books on shelves, rearranging the Cozy Corgi merchandise section, or simply cleaning. It pleased me to see him taking a moment to himself.

Having had the fill of gossip the day before, after the bakery's morning rush had passed, there'd not been many people in. Which worked for me. I'd planned on making headway on Nadiya's case, but... I just wasn't.

Maybe feeling my attention, Watson looked up from where he'd been curled at Ben's feet. He cocked his head in that inquisitive way of his, got up, gave an exaggerated stretch with his nubbed tail of a rump in the air, then plodded toward me.

Ben glanced down at the movement, his gaze following Watson's path, then offered me one of his shy smiles before returning to his notebook.

Watson looked at me expectantly when he reached the edge of the sofa.

"I don't have any t-r-e-a-t-s, if that's what you're hoping for." Watson was a smart old soul. If I wasn't careful, he'd learn the spelling of his favorite word, but as we hadn't crossed that bridge yet, the letters didn't elicit any frantic exuberance. Shifting the computer slightly so I could bend, I stroked his head.

Watson pressed his cheek into my palm.

My heart melted a little. "How do you do that? You're such a grumpy little thing, but you always know when my mind or soul is heavy, don't you?"

He twisted slightly so I had no choice but to scratch down his spine.

I chuckled. "I guess you get something out of it too, though, don't you?" With a final pat, I repositioned myself back on the sofa. I expected Watson to return to Ben's side, but to my surprise, he waddled a few steps closer to the fire, plopped down with a contented sigh, and cast me an unusually adoring glance before he closed his eyes.

Katie came down the steps, catching my attention just as I was about to return to the computer screen. She crossed the room to Ben, gave him a baked item, then headed directly to me, not needing to look around—I was a creature of habit, after all.

She handed me a twisted knot of bread as she sat down beside me. "Here, I tried a new variation once the breakfast rush stopped. These just came out of the oven." She laughed when Watson raised his head and whimpered. After tearing off a small section of her own roll, she tossed it to him.

He caught it, chewed, then lowered his head once more and fell back to sleep.

I shook my head at his laziness. "He really does think he's king of the world, doesn't he?"

"Isn't he?" Katie motioned toward the roll. "Well, try it. I'm pretty pleased and considering adding it as a staple as one of our savory selections. Do you think the horseradish is too much?"

"As if anything you do is ever too much." I motioned toward her sweater, which depicted a turkey wearing a Santa hat. "Except for your clothing choices. We just decorated for Thanksgiving yesterday, and you're already moving on to Christmas."

"Technically it's the holiday season—they all blend together. And as long as it's got a turkey on it, I think it's fair game. And don't get me started on the drab, baby-poo color palette of your wardrobe." She motioned to the roll again. "Well?"

I took a bite of it and instantly rolled my eyes back in my head as a groan escaped. Katie could say whatever she wanted about my wardrobe as long as she kept feeding me these. The sharp sting of the horseradish blended perfectly with Katie's new obsession of the bread with garlic in the dough. The sharp cheddar she'd folded inside was still melty, and the meat was crispy.

"I thought the black-forest ham gave it a little extra bite, as well as more salt to combine with the cheese, which goes well with the creaminess of the horseradish. The subtle underflavor of the garlic ties it all together." She took her own bite and nodded before talking with her mouth full. "I don't think the horseradish is too much. It burns your nose just a touch."

Following her lead, I took another bite, larger that time, and didn't bother swallowing. "I don't know about the burn, but this thing is heaven. At this rate, I'm okay if you use this garlicky bread for everything else you create from this point on."

She laughed again. "I'll use it as the crust on the next batch of lemon bars and see if you still say that."

I shuddered at the thought. Although, if anyone could pull it off, it would be Katie.

We polished off the rest of our rolls before she spoke again, this time concern lacing her words. "Are you hurting about Branson?"

I'd slept in that morning, trying to recoup from my exhaustion and only had a few moments before opening to fill Katie in on the events of the previous night.

"No." I reconsidered. "Maybe a little, at least in the back of my mind. We wouldn't have worked out. I have no doubt of that. I'm glad I didn't allow things to go further. It wouldn't have been fair to either of us, but I did hope we'd settle into friendship. But... I don't think that's going to happen. At least not with the strain of Chief Briggs's vendetta against me."

Katie let out a growl that almost resembled Watson's. "What is that about anyway? Talk about unfounded bias."

I shrugged but didn't reply. Branson had been right. Though my father would've handled things with more respect and in a smoother manner than Chief Briggs, I had no doubt he would've felt the same about a civilian doing what I was doing. Granted, I also knew he would've seen me as the exception, but that would have been because I was his daughter and he had faith in me. Chief Briggs had no such ties.

Though it had played around the periphery of my thoughts and emotions all morning, talking about it brought Branson front and center, which wasn't helpful or fun, so I shoved it back. "He's not who I've been thinking about this morning." I angled the computer so Katie could see the screen. "Since we couldn't dig up anything about our poacher brothers last night, I figured I'd start with Nadiya, try to discover a lead that would help clear her name." I sighed. "I'm finding just the opposite."

Katie's brown eyes widened as she straightened and scooted closer. "Really? What have you found?"

"Nothing that links her to the poachers, obviously, but quite a few things that make me think she might be capable of what Branson said. Just a scroll through her Facebook page was quite enlightening." I slid my finger over the track pad of the laptop, slow enough that Katie could read the comments on Nadiya's social media posts.

"Wow!" Katie lowered to a whisper as her eyes skimmed the screen. "Leo wasn't kidding about her being passionate. Granted, a lot of these aren't things she wrote herself, just memes that she's shared from other pages."

True enough. "Maybe so, but if she's sharing them, they obviously match how she feels." I scrolled a little further until I found a post from a couple of weeks before. "Check this one out."

The image was a cartoon of an elephant and rhinoceros sitting in high-backed armchairs in front of a fireplace. On the walls around them were the mounted heads of humans, each wearing a variety of hunters' hats. Above the image, Nadiya had typed, *If only every poacher could get what they deserved. How I'd love to visit a room like this.*

Katie grimaced. "Wow. That's..." She cocked her head, reminding me of Watson only moments before. "Although, if it weren't for the murder yesterday, would you really think twice about this? It doesn't seem that out of character for a park ranger to feel this way."

"Maybe so." I'd considered that as well. "If it was just one or two, but, Katie"—I met her gaze—"this goes on for months and months, posts like these. It's not just once when she was angry or something. Almost all of her social media accounts follow this line of shares and comments."

"Sure, but like I said, she's a park ranger, and..." Katie shook her head and let out a heavy sigh. "But I can't see Leo posting things like this. Maybe a comic like that every once in a while, but never with the hate and the tone of the comments that she's demonstrating. And we both know how angry and passionate Leo can get about poaching."

I nodded. "That's where I'm coming from as well. And..." I clicked on another tab. "Look at all the groups she belongs to. All of them are animal-rights groups, which isn't bad, obviously, but a lot of them are extremist." I judged Katie's expression before clicking one more tab. "And then there's this."

Katie read for several moments before she let out another sigh and leaned back against the couch. "That's public record?"

I nodded again. "Yeah. And it came up pretty quickly, so chances are there's more." I'd found three separate arrests on Nadiya's record. Two charges of assault. "She wasn't convicted on any of them, but... they're there, *multiple* charges. And that suggests a pattern."

Katie blinked, suddenly looking tired. "Still, we're talking murder here."

"Patterns escalate. Most people don't just wake up and decide to kill someone out of the blue."

"You know that's not how it always works." She sounded skeptical. "We've seen it ourselves enough lately—crimes of passion where someone wasn't planning on murdering someone. They just... do, or whatever."

"That's not what it was with Max." Though it hadn't shaken me, I could picture Athena and me discovering his body perfectly. "He was shot right between the eyes, and his body was specifically taken to the statues of the sheep. It was intentional."

Katie was unusually silent for a moment, then shrugged. "I can't argue with that. It doesn't mean Nadiya is guilty, but..."

"There's one more thing." I clicked on the final tab, which opened to a link on Nadiya's Twitter feed.

Katie leaned forward once more and then groaned. She looked at the picture of the beautiful woman holding up a blue ribbon in one hand and a rifle in the other. "She's a master marksman."

"Yep. Seems kind of strange to me that someone so against hunting would be skilled with the gun."

"For self-defense?" The false hope in Katie's tone was clear.

I tapped the blue ribbon. "That's not what this says to me."

"No. Me neither."

"It all adds up to a pretty incriminating picture." I shut the laptop, feeling sick. "All abstract and nothing definitive, obviously. But when you put it together with what Branson told me last night, that she was arrested *in* her truck, *with* the murder weapon, and blood and mud that looked like drag marks in her truck bed, it would've been negligent for the police *not* to charge her with Max's murder."

"No kidding." Just as she was about to sink farther into the sofa, Katie straightened once more, her eyes brightening. "But from what you've said, that Max guy was huge. Nadiya is built like a cheerleader. You saw her in that pink panther getup. How in the world could she drag a man that size?"

And again, I'd thought the same thing. "Cheerleaders are strong, and I bet most park rangers are too." Then I went a step further. "And... maybe... she didn't do it by herself. Though if she was caught driving away from dropping off Max's body at Sheep Island, you'd think whoever helped would still be with her."

Katie gaped at me.

"What?" I saw accusation in her eyes.

"The way you're talking. It sounds like you've decided that Leo is wrong, that Nadiya did kill Max."

"No, I haven't. I..." I paused, considering. "Maybe I have." Clearly I did. Though I'd not let myself solidify that thought. But it would explain the sick feeling in my gut.

I waited for Katie to argue, to offer some other explanation, but she didn't. Finally she gestured toward the closed computer. "Do you think Leo knows all of this?"

"I was wondering about that. It's hard to imagine that he does and for him not to bring any of it up last night." I hated the way I was thinking. "Unless he was trying to protect Nadiya."

Katie shook her head instantly, her curls flying. "No way. If Leo thought she did this, he wouldn't cover for her. *And*, he respects you, *believes* in you. If he knew all of this, there's no way he'd ask you to investigate. I mean"—she gestured at the computer again—"you found this in a matter of minutes. He knows you're not an idiot." Some of her dogmatism faded, leaving her sad. "He's going to be devastated."

"Are they together... romantically?" I hadn't really planned on asking, but the answer would affect things.

Katie's brows furrowed. "Who?"

"Leo and Nadiya?" I tried to keep the *isn't that obvious* out of my tone and failed.

"No. Absolutely not." Again with the headshake and then once more with the shoulder slump. "I mean... I did consider it the other night when I met Nadiya for the first time. The way she looks, she'd be hard for any man to ignore. And she and Leo have the whole love-of-nature thing in common. But... no, I don't think he's looking at anyone else like that."

Anyone else? That was as close as Katie had ever gotten to confirming my suspicions that there was something going on between the two of them. I put my hand on her knee. "Are you sure you're not just seeing what you want to see?"

She looked at me, puzzled. "Surely you don't think Leo had anything to do with this."

I flinched. "No, of course not. I mean..." It was time to rip off the Band-Aid. I'd been wondering for months, been getting mixed signals and clues from both of them. Might as well get all cards on the table. "It's okay, you don't have to hide it anymore. I know you and Leo are together, that you've been trying to keep it under wraps, probably not wanting me to feel like the third wheel. So it makes sense you may not want to think he has ulterior motives as far as Nadiya is concerned, but I think we have to..." My words trailed off at the expression of utter bafflement on her face.

"What are you talking about? Leo and I aren't together." Katie shuddered. "Gross. I love him, but he's my brother. Well... *like* a brother, obviously. But we've never..." She shuddered again. "Gross!"

There was no doubt that Katie was being completely honest, and I just stared at her. I'd been so sure. Well, no, I hadn't been, but there'd been moments. "Katie, Leo calls you all these endearments—sweetie, honey, all that kind of stuff. The way he looks at you, and he rubs your shoulders or touches your arm. He only does that with you, not with me. You're special."

She rolled her eyes. "And you're an idiot."

I flinched again. "What?"

"He's only had eyes for you since the moment he met you. You know that."

"No. He..." Why was I denying it? Leo had made it very clear he had feelings for me when we met. I'd had them for him. "Katie, that was months ago. And it ended nearly a year ago. As soon as it looked like Branson and I were... whatever we were doing..."

"Exactly." This time, Katie grabbed my knee. "You know Leo—he was doing the gentlemanly thing. He expressed interest—you said you wanted friendship. So... that's what he gave you."

I sat there dumbfounded. Though, in truth, I was only partially dumbfounded. Just like there had been moments that I'd observed with him and Katie— though he never called me any sweet names or touched me in the way he did Katie—there'd still been moments... where I felt something between us, some tension, something... I'd shoved it away, ignored it.

Katie released my knee but gave it a couple of pats before she pulled her hand away. "I really thought you knew."

I didn't answer. I couldn't.

She leaned a little closer, tilting her head so her hair fell in a short curtain around her shoulders. "Do you also not know that *you* have feelings for *him*?"

"Katie, I do not. I…" Couldn't finish that statement either, it seemed. Maybe I did. There was no *maybe* about it; I knew I did. But I'd been shoving those away and ignoring them with a passion that rivaled Nadiya's social media posts.

Katie stretched out her hand and tapped one of the earrings that were made up of a chain of silver corgis Leo had given me on the opening night of the bookshop. "You never take these off."

Dear Lord, I really was an idiot.

Branson had pointed out the same thing about the earrings months ago. But I'd told him, and myself, that it was because Leo was a friend and because I loved corgis. All of which was true. But there was more to it than that.

I met Katie's gaze, and she chuckled and smiled sadly. "Oh, Fred. How many bodies have you stumbled across? And I don't think I've ever seen you look quite as terrified as you do right now."

It was a true statement. So very, very true. "I… I don't know what to do with any of this."

She shrugged. "Who says you have to do anything with it? At least right now."

"But, Leo..."

"Leo's fine." She smiled. "He's head over heels for you, but he's fine. He's sweet and kind, but he's also strong. And while maybe he's not pursuing anyone else, he's also not putting his life on pause for you either." She shrugged. "That's part of why I was wondering if maybe he was moving on when I saw Nadiya. I don't think he is, but... I suppose there's a chance."

I most definitely did not know what to do with *that*.

So I shoved it away as well. As always, I focused on what I did much better than feelings and romantic relationships. "First things first. Nadiya. Gotta figure her out."

Though Katie clucked her tongue and shook her head, her voice brightened. "Of course." She gave a little chuckle and stood, waking Watson in the process. "Where are you going to start?"

Leo was probably the best place to begin, but pushing the other matter aside or not, I wasn't quite ready to cross that bridge. So I'd start with second best. "Delilah." I stood and smoothed out my skirt. "However, I think I'm going to require fortification in the way of another one of those heavenly rolls you just made, and another dirty chai." I turned to Watson. "Come on, buddy. Delilah loves you, so *we've* got work to do. I'll even give you a treat in prepayment."

Though he'd been blinking heavy eyes, at his favorite word, he brightened, gave a little happy yip, a hop, and hurried over to the base of the stairs, prancing back and forth as he turned toward Katie and me, clearly wondering why we were moving so slowly.

After a second of Katie's heaven-filled garlic rolls and a dirty chai, I left the Cozy Corgi. With Watson at my side, I reminded myself that I was well-slept, well-fed, well-caffeinated and accompanied by my not-so-secret-weapon of fur, grump, and cuteness. I might have some personal qualms with Delilah Johnson, but they were just that—*personal*. They shouldn't interfere if she could possibly help me clear an innocent woman from murder charges. Or... interfere in getting facts that might help Leo accept that his friend and coworker—or secret crush, *whatever* she was to him—was guilty.

Bundled in my jacket, scarf, and positive self-talk, we crossed to the other side of Elkhorn Avenue. I'd anticipated seeing Anna and Carl Hanson in the window of Cabin and Hearth, always ready and waiting for gossip to enter their front door, but instead, noticed Jetsam sitting behind the glass door of Paws, staring at us forlornly. I gave the redheaded corgi a finger wave and kept going.

Within four steps, I was pulled to an abrupt halt by Watson's leash. I looked back only to find him straining to get to Jetsam.

The sight was enough to make me wonder if I'd overdosed on caffeine and was seeing things. I dismissed the notion quickly. It was impossible to have too much caffeine. Clearly I'd simply not had enough.

Watson gave another tug and pulled me closer to the pet shop. To my utter amazement, when I followed him, Watson pressed his nose against the glass. Jetsam mimicked his gesture.

"You actually want to go in there?" I thought I was pretty good at understanding what Watson desired at all times, but I had to be misreading things. True, he and Paulie's two crazy corgis had formed... not a friendship, more an understanding that led to mutual respect, but never in a million years would I have believed Watson might initiate contact.

Watson glanced back at me with a pitiful whimper, then turned around with another tug. Clearly he wanted to keep me guessing.

"Okay, then." I shrugged and headed toward the door. "Remember you brought this on yourself."

When we walked into Paws, Jetsam not only didn't go insane at the sight of Watson, he barely moved. I had to lift my skirt to keep from tripping as I stepped over him. And while there was the ever present bubbling of aquariums, squawk of birds, and whirl of hamster wheels, there was no onslaught of barking from the back, no rush of Flotsam hurrying through the shop to meet us.

When I noticed Pearl wandering over from a couple of feet away, I decided she was the reason Watson had demanded we stop in. However, after a quick greeting to her, Watson pressed his nose to Jetsam's just as he had through the window and then nearly bowled me over when he gave the other corgi a lick.

"Oh, hey, Winifred." I'd been so distracted by the dogs, I'd not even bothered to look toward the counter, where Paulie gave me a weak smile and sounded nearly as forlorn as Jetsam looked. Athena was with him behind the counter, and if I wasn't mistaken, was just pulling back from an embrace.

I gave another quick glance toward the dogs. With Pearl nuzzled against him, Watson had laid down beside Jetsam, their backs pressed together.

Baffled, I released my hold on his leash and turned back to my friends. "Hi. Sorry to interrupt. We were walking by and Watson practically demanded we stop in."

"Did he?" Paulie's voice shook, and a tear rolled down his cheek. "He must've known."

Athena lifted a hand and rubbed his back.

The only possibility slammed into me. Paulie clearly upset, Jetsam heartbroken, and Watson acting in a very un-Watson-like manner. Even so, I took a final glance around the shop, hoping to be proven wrong. But no chubby, tricolored corgi emerged. I almost couldn't bring myself to ask. "Is Flotsam…?" No, I *couldn't* bring myself to ask if he was dead. I just couldn't.

Paulie nodded, started to speak, then sucked in a breath and got lost to tears.

Athena shifted so her arm went all the way around him and pulled Paulie into her side as she spoke softly to me. "Flotsam got really sick this morning, apparently. He's at the vet. Paulie called me a little while ago, and I came right down."

It wasn't what I'd expected to hear, so it took a moment to process. "He's sick?"

Paulie's bloodshot brown eyes flashed up at me.

I realized I'd sound relieved and adjusted my

tone as I hurried forward. "Paulie, I'm so sorry. I know how horrible it is when one of our babies is sick." I reached over the counter and placed my hand on his, rubbing him as Athena continued to hold him tight. "What's wrong with him?"

Paulie shook his head, and though he slammed his eyes shut, a fresh wave of tears began.

Athena cast him a hesitant glance, then refocused on me. "They're not sure. From what Paulie says, it sounds like it was really sudden. They're wondering if he got into something poisonous or"—she cast another look at Paulie, and her tone became questioning—"if he might've had a stroke?" When Paulie nodded, she continued, "Sounds like Flotsam has to stay at the clinic for tests to be run and remain under observation until he's stable."

Paulie nodded again in confirmation.

Most of my relief faded at the dire news, and with a grateful look back at Watson, who was still cuddled up with Jetsam and Pearl, I released Paulie's hand so I could make my way around the counter and wrap him in a hug as well.

Paulie broke, sobbing and shaking, and my heart broke right along with him. His corgis might still drive me the tiniest bit insane, but I'd grown fond of them, and Paulie had become a dear friend. I knew he loved his boys as much as I loved Watson. Athena and I exchanged sorrowful glances. Though they didn't fall, tears glistened on her long dark lashes.

I didn't know how much time passed, but we stayed that way until Paulie calmed and his breathing returned to normal. Finally, once more under control, he gave himself a shake and cleared his throat. "I shouldn't break down like this. I need to believe that things are going to be fine. I'm just so..." His trembling fingers reached out and grasped the edge of the counter for support, but he didn't finish speaking.

Athena had resumed rubbing Paulie's back, and though she addressed me, her gaze remained on him. "I was about to contact you earlier, Fred, when I got Paulie's call." When he gave a small nod, Athena focused on me. "I haven't been able to find anything revolutionary about Sid or Eddie, at least nothing that wasn't already public knowledge. In fact, there's not a single report or article that connects the two of them. Which, we know that they were. You said yourself that their relationship had soured when Sid changed their agreement on the drug distribution. So you already know more than what I could find."

"I was afraid of that." I too glanced at Paulie, making sure he was okay to talk about other things.

His tears had stopped, so I took that as a good sign. Maybe puzzling over other things would distract him. "We've not been able to find anything either. Although, since you and I found Max's body, I switched to researching him and his brother instead of Sid and Eddie. But I'm not having any luck there either."

Athena's gaze turned shrewd. "Well, that's what's interesting." She grimaced. "Not interesting, so much as *frustrating*. I've been looking into them as well, of course. It's been a day and a half since you and I discovered his body. That's why I was going to contact you a little bit ago, because the police finally released his last name. They claimed they were having trouble getting in contact with the nearest kin to give notice of death. Someone other than his brother, obviously. But I don't believe it took that long."

"I'm afraid that's my fault." I felt a flicker of my temper ignite, which was preferable to the sorrow and worry over Flotsam. "It's hardly a secret that Susan and Chief Briggs don't appreciate me looking into murders." *And occasionally Branson*—I kept that thought to myself. "It seems that Briggs has decided to make things as difficult as possible for me to do so."

I started to fill them in on Branson's and my

conversation, but it felt too personal in a way. And considering Paulie's state, also a bit inappropriate.

"As you know, Chief Briggs considers Paulie part of my *Scooby Gang*, as he calls us." I glanced at Paulie, hoping for a flicker of a smile. He'd been so lonely and desperate for friends, I'd hoped the reference would bring him a bit of happiness. He only winced. "He knows how close you and Paulie are, Athena, so I would imagine he assumes anything you know, I will know."

She nodded. "I guarantee that you're right." She shrugged. "Although, I can't let you take *all* the credit. You know firsthand that I've historically not had the best relationship with a few of the higher-powered members of the town council. Chief Briggs is most definitely in their pocket, and vice versa. There's never been any love lost between him and me."

"With the vacancies that have opened up recently, I hope that will be changing." Two members of the town council had been murdered a few months ago.

"Dream on." Athena waved me off. "Anyway, Max's last name is Weasel. So Max and Jim Weasel."

I cocked an eyebrow. "Weasel?"

She chuckled. "Yep, can't make these things up.

But I've not had the chance to see what I can find out about them. I quite literally just got the call right before I came down here."

"Well... it's a place to start." And more than I had before.

I was tempted to bring up Nadiya, see if either of them had any interactions with her and be able to share something that might be enlightening, ask Athena to do some deeper research on her as well, but it seemed rather cold to keep going when Paulie was rightfully so upset. Chances were low he'd had much interaction with Nadiya. I knew Delilah found Paulie rather repulsive, and if Nadiya was part of her new Pink Panthers club, I figured she would feel similarly. I could always call Athena later to see if she'd mind adding another name to her research.

When I became aware that we'd been quiet for an awkwardly long time, I glanced at three curled-up dogs and decided I'd done all I could do. I pulled Paulie into another quick hug. "I'm so sorry, sweetie. Let me know the minute you have an update. I'm sure Flotsam will be back to his crazy self in no time."

Paulie choked out a wet-sounding laugh and nodded into my shoulder.

"In the meantime, let me know if you need anything, you hear? Anything at all."

Another nod, and then he released me.

Before I stepped away, I gave Athena's hand a squeeze, and she nodded.

When I picked up Watson's leash and he nuzzled Pearl goodbye and gave a goodbye lick to Jetsam, I felt tears threaten once more.

TEN

My thoughts were still on Paulie and Flotsam as Watson and I walked the short distance to Old Tyme Photography. The thought of one of Paulie's dogs being sick made me hurt for my friend, but also made me fear for Watson. The concept of loss and knowing that a solitary day could make such an impactful change on a life had been driven home years ago by my father's murder, but it was a fact that I did my best to ignore as much as possible. I assumed most people did as well. If we kept that front and center, who would be able to function?

I blamed those heavy thoughts for both causing me to bump into someone when I entered the photography shop and for not recognizing the woman instantly. I didn't get a chance to apologize before Delilah's voice drew my attention.

The stunning redhead was behind an old-fashioned camera at the far end of the narrow shop, with a family of four—consisting of a mother, father, toddler daughter, and infant son—all dressed in black-and-white striped prison garb and standing behind a false wall of bars. Delilah turned from the camera and waved. "Watson, darling! I'm so thrilled you came to see me." She lifted her blue eyes to me, and I caught a playful glint. "And you too, Fred. Please don't leave—let me wrap up here. I've been meaning to talk to you." The glint faded slightly. "Although, there appears to be a line for the pleasure of my presence."

Unsure what to say, I just gave a little wave back.

Delilah returned her attention to the family. "Now remember, you're in the slammer. You're supposed to look serious and depressed." She took on a flirtatious tone. "And, Mr. Porter, the camera loves you, but if you can't quit giggling, you're going to ruin the shoot."

"Please keep your filthy animal away. I'd rather it not urinate on my shoe."

At the sneer from the woman beside me, I glanced down at Watson, who was merely sniffing the hem of the woman's skirt. I pulled his leash just a touch tighter. "Watson is house-trained. I promise you he won't..." My words fell away as I looked up into the thin face of Ethel Beaker. We'd not had any interaction before, but she'd inserted herself in the top slot of the town council after her husband had been killed, and her daughter-in-law and I had never seen eye to eye. I cleared my throat. "Sorry that I bumped into you. I was a little distracted."

"I noticed." She sidestepped farther and lifted her nose in the air.

A tense silence fell between us. I should've counted that as a blessing, as it was certainly preferable to anything Ethel would have to say to me. But being who I was, my tongue seemed to work on its own accord, more concerned about filling the void than common sense. "How's Carla and..." I drew a complete blank on Carla's husband and baby's names. "I haven't seen her in months, not since..." For as much as my tongue wanted to talk, it was doing a rather remarkable job of not finishing a thought. Though, that was probably wise.

Ethel cocked a severely shaped eyebrow. "Since she shut down her coffee shop in shame? The location of my husband's death?" She sniffed. "Since then?"

I felt my cheeks burn, and I wished that Watson would prove me wrong and urinate on her shoe, or mine, or anything that would provide distraction.

"Yes... since... around that time, yes." And then, by some supernatural power of awkwardness given to all booklovers, I kept going. "I've noticed that there's no For Sale sign or anything in the windows of Black Bear Roaster. Is Carla hoping to reopen?"

Ethel's other eyebrow came up to the higher level of the first. If I wasn't wrong, she almost looked impressed with my ability to stick my foot in my mouth. "Worried about competition?"

"No. No, of course not. It's just..." I realized how that sounded. And though it was true, at least in terms of bakery items—there was no competition between the prepackaged stuff Carla had served and the carby bits of heaven Katie crafted—I bit my tongue, finally, and refocused on Watson.

He was smirking. Although he might've simply had a spot of flatulence, I wasn't really sure, but I was willing to bet he was smirking.

And, *dear Lord*, was Delilah ever going to get done with the photo shoot?

I thought that Ethel Beaker and I were done talking, that we'd reached an implied agreement to keep things unspoken. But she suddenly shifted toward me once more, leaning her elaborately dressed elbow on the glass countertop. "And you, Winifred? How are you finding our little town? Business going well?"

Her tone had taken on a friendly, conversational quality that elicited fear. Unable to find the trap, or a way out, I answered honestly. "I'm loving it. Estes Park is the most beautiful place in the world, and I'm surrounded by wonderful people and a store full of books... not to mention pastries. What more could a girl want?"

Ethel's smile grew. "From what I've observed, it seems pretty clear what you're after."

"Oh?" I'd already been certain I was wading into quicksand, but if there'd been any doubt, that rushed it away. I truly couldn't fathom where she was leading, outside of the looking into murders.

She nodded. "I've heard through the rumor mill that you're a divorcée."

Okay, definitely not about murders. I simply nodded.

Ethel leaned forward slightly, as if getting ready to gossip with a girlfriend. "I can't blame you for looking for a replacement. Estes Park has its share of eligible, handsome bachelors." Her gaze flicked toward Delilah. "And I suppose some that are neither eligible nor bachelors, but still."

I swallowed, wished I could think of a way to stop wherever this was leading, but the only thing that came to mind was turning tail and running as fast as I could to the door. Pride, stupidly, held me in place.

"Interesting thing is, you—" When she looked back at me, her gaze traveled slowly down my body and back up, leaving no question that she found me lacking "—caught the crown jewel. The man every woman in town had been longing for and throwing themselves after, to be quite honest."

Branson. *That's* where we were going. "I wasn't trying to catch anything, Ms. Beaker."

Her smile turned wicked. "Come now, we both know better. What I can't understand is why in the world a woman like you"—she gave yet another flick down my body—"would risk playing such a dangerous game with a man so completely out of her league." She chuckled. "But then again... it's working, isn't it? You've got our dashing sergeant wrapped around your finger. No one gave you enough credit. You're just as much of a manipulating temptress as this jezebel over here." Without looking away, she cocked her head toward Delilah.

I was almost relieved at the place we'd landed. It allowed my indignation to ignite my temper. "I can assure you, none of what you're saying is factual, nor... is it any of your business."

The second the words left my lips, I realized my mistake. I'd given her exactly what she wanted.

Ethel leaned in for the kill, her voice cold and filled with disgust. "You think you're so much better than everyone else, don't you? Let me tell you something, *you're not*. And one day, hopefully sooner rather than later, Sergeant Wexler will wake up and realize that he's a much higher caliber of person than you are. You're arrogant, abrasive, entitled, and nothing more than a joke. The whole town has watched you yank a good man back and forth as you've dragged his affection through the mud. And soon he'll wake up and realize that he can do so, *so* much better than the likes of you."

"Let me guess, that someone better would be *you?*" From out of nowhere, Delilah appeared between us on the other side of the counter and smiled sweetly at Ethel. "Darling, if Winifred is out of Branson's league, then you are on a completely different planet. And..." She leaned forward, mimicking the position Ethel had taken only moments before, and when she gave her version of the wicked smile, she made it clear that she was the master between the two of them. "Talk about robbing the cradle. I know you must spend a small fortune on moisturizer, but just between us girls, it's not *that* good."

"You sleazy, hateful..." Ethel bristled and drew herself up to her full height before glancing over at the tourist family who were changing their children back into their normal clothes. When she spoke again, she was under control. "I won't take much of your time, Miss Johnson. I simply came here to tell you that if you insist on continuing gang behavior, it will be brought up at the town council and ordinances will have to be passed. Ones with financial or licensure consequences, or both."

Delilah started to retort, then blinked. "I have no idea what you're talking about. Gang behavior?"

"I'm surrounded by imbeciles." Ethel pointed to a pink silk jacket that was thrown over a chair a few feet away. White embroidery over the back read *Pink Panthers*, and just the topmost portion of a similarly embroidered panther head was visible. "You and your gang of hussies, roaming the streets of our town all wearing the same outfit of your exclusive club? That looks like gang behavior to me."

Delilah looked from Ethel to the jacket, then back again. Her expression revealed utter bewilderment, then shock, and then she threw back her head and laughed. Finally she looked back at Ethel.

"What's the matter, you old witch? Jealous your application into the club got rejected?"

"As if I'd ever—"

She pointed to the door. "Get out of my shop." All humor left Delilah's eyes and tone. If I'd ever wondered if Delilah was capable of murder, all doubts fled. "You have three seconds before I throw you out myself."

To my surprise, Ethel moved instantly, but her tone didn't waver as she gave a dark hiss. "Remember, you've made your choice. You'll have to live with the consequences. Might want to check your mail for an official notification."

"Do that, please! I've been wanting to throw some money at a lawyer." She waved at Ethel's retreating form, and then with a smile as sweet as candy, she turned back to the tourists who were staring wide-eyed from their pace at the counter. "And that's why you'll see the signs that say don't feed the wildlife. They can turn rabid and try to take over the town."

The family chuckled awkwardly, paid for their order, and agreed to come back in a couple of hours to pick up their tintype photograph souvenirs.

Finally, Delilah looked at me, and when she did, all pretense left her features and voice. She almost sounded as if we were friends when she spoke. "What did you do to her? I figured she worshiped the ground you walked on. Didn't you solve her husband's murder?"

"I did. Yes. But…" I shrugged. "I assumed she hated me because of Carla. I had no idea she had feelings about Branson."

Delilah waved me off with a laugh. "Oh please, it's no secret that Ethel hates her daughter-in-law more than she could possibly hate you. And as far as Branson"—she shrugged—"I don't really know what that's about. I can't imagine she actually has any designs on ensnaring him for herself, but she isn't wrong. After all the women who've tried to capture Branson's affections, it's a scandal that you're the one who succeeded. And even more so that you know how to play him like a fiddle." She cast a similar appraising glance over me as Ethel had before, but there was no disgust or judgment behind her eyes. If anything, she seemed impressed. "I say, go you! Woman power!" She shook her fist in the air with a laugh.

Though it was a completely different reaction, it was the same interpretation. "I am *not* trying to play him like a fiddle. Nor am I trying to jerk him around. I don't understand why people keep insinuating that.

We've gone on some dates. That's all. That's what dating is, to decide if you're compatible, decide if you're meant to be together and make a good team. Sometimes that's clear instantly, and others, like... with us... it takes a while to figure out."

When Delilah smiled, there was no teasing or any of her normal edge. "That's actually how it is with you, isn't it?" She didn't wait for a response and patted my hand. "I knew I liked you. You're real. And while we're very different people, you and me, we have a couple things in common. We're blunt, and we're smart. And we don't pretend to be anything other than what we are." She pointed her thumb over at the jacket. "Any chance you'd like to be a Pink Panther?"

I nearly choked. "Are you serious?"

She nodded. "Very."

Despite myself, some middle school part of me was flattered. I'd just been invited to sit at the cool girls' table. It only took a moment to remember my qualms with Delilah Johnson. "That's kind of you. But no. Thank you. As I'm sure you've noticed, I have my hands full right now."

She surprised me a second time when I noticed a flash of genuine hurt in her beautiful blue eyes. "I don't meet your standards, yes, I know." She sloughed off whatever hurt she felt as easily as I imagined she made the men she wanted fall at her feet. "But that's okay. You meet mine in a lot of ways." As if putting on battle armor, she walked over, lifted the jacket off the chair, and slipped into it, before walking around the counter and kneeling in front of Watson. "Sorry, hot stuff. Wasn't trying to ignore you."

As before, Watson didn't lose his mind over her but seemed to thoroughly enjoy her attention without the promise of a treat.

I couldn't help myself. "So that jacket isn't part of the Halloween costume. Your group actually wears them all the time?"

Without taking her attention off Watson, she nodded. "We do. I'm surprised you haven't seen us wearing them around town. I was always obsessed with the movie *Grease* and wanted to be a Pink Lady. This is my version. Personally, I think it's better. Panthers are sexy."

I couldn't figure her out, and I discovered I rather enjoyed that aspect of Delilah. Despite my personal judgments of how she chose to engage in her affairs, her quite literal affairs, I found myself liking the woman. "Well, I didn't know about the jackets, but I did know about your group, and that's why I'm here, because Nadiya was one of you, right?"

"*Was?*" Delilah looked up, stroked Watson another couple of seconds, and then stood. "Nadiya *is* a Pink Panther. She's not dead. And she's why I wanted to come see you, obviously. I figured Leo was going to ask you to look into Nadiya's innocence. And honestly, as much as it seems you enjoy showing the police that you can outsmart them, I figured it wouldn't take much, if any, convincing." She leaned against the counter as Ethel had before but without the feeling she was laying a trap.

"I'm not trying to show the police that I—"

"None of that. It wasn't an insult." She cut me off and gave me a meaningful stare. "I'm sure that your main reason is because you wanted to clear several people important to you. But don't pretend that you don't enjoy getting the job done. Especially when we all know that certain members of the police force and the town council don't like you sticking your nose in the middle of things."

As much as I wanted to deny her accusation, I couldn't. It was true. And from her tone, it wasn't really an accusation. "Okay, then, I am looking into Nadiya, but everything I've found about her makes her look guilty. Honestly, it seems like the police are on the right track."

Delilah scowled, and an offended quality entered her husky voice. "Why? Because she's passionate about animal rights? Because she's been in the police's face about all the poaching in the few months that she's been here?"

"No. It's because…" I was about to list the litany of reasons I'd found on the internet and to tell her the things Branson had confided to me about the night Nadiya was arrested, then thought better of it. "*You* wanted to see me, Delilah. Was it only to ask me to look into it? You said yourself, you already figured I was. So why did you really want to see me? Do you have any proof of Nadiya's innocence? You were with her that night, you and all the Pink Ladies were going around for Halloween, right? Can you or one of your group be her alibi?"

Her defensiveness fell away, and she shook her head in defeat. "No. We all split up after." For the second time, she touched my hand. Just when I thought she was about to pull away, she slipped her fingers around and held on. "What I said before was true. I do like you. I think you're smart, and I think you're honest. And I truly believe you're trying to help people, even if you do get a kick out of outsmarting the cops." Her lips twitched into what started to be a smile, but then she grew serious once more. "I'm sure of what you found on the internet. I know Nadiya's past. I know what she's passionate about. I know all the reasons she looks guilty. And I don't have one solitary thing to give you to say that she isn't. I wish to God I did. I'd be giving it to you, to the police, to whoever. But I don't."

That wasn't what I was expecting. Not at all. "Nothing? Then why did you want to see me?"

"Because I'm scared. For that very reason, the fact that I can't give you anything scares me. It's true Nadiya's only been here a short while, but she's become a very dear and trusted friend. She's become family to me, and the Pink Panthers are all the family she has. If you knew her, you'd love her."

Maybe she was right. Judging from the way Leo felt about her, it seemed to be an effect Nadiya had on people. Some of Delilah's words rang in my mind. "What do you mean the Pink Panthers are all the family she has?" Now that she mentioned it, I realized I'd not seen a single family connection on social media.

Delilah balked as if caught off guard, but hardened instantly. "That's Nadiya's business and has nothing to do with this."

"Maybe you're wrong. Anything you tell me might lead me to proving her innocence."

"It won't." She relaxed somewhat. "Listen, Fred, I just need to know that you're not going to give up. No matter what else you uncover about her or whatever *proof* you think you find that she did this, just keep looking. And if you need my help, I will do anything—*anything*. I'd be doing it now if I could think of something." She gave a sad laugh and shrugged once more. "Well, I guess I am. This is the only thing I thought of—begging you. She's innocent. I'd bet my life on it. But I also know that if you don't prove it, she'll go to jail for murder. When even her friends can't offer anything to clear her name, I don't know how I can rightly expect the police to think anything different than what they already do, especially when they already had a grudge against her to begin with." She was squeezing my hand so hard it nearly hurt. "But they're wrong, Fred. I swear to you. They are."

Watson curled up in the passenger seat of the Mini Cooper as we drove out of downtown Estes Park. And though I didn't mention Leo's name, Watson must've been able to sense him, as he sat up straighter the closer we got to the national park. By the time the tollbooths, which resembled tiny narrow log cabins, at the entrance to Rocky Mountain National Park came into view, Watson had both forepaws perched on the passenger door and craned his head to see through the windshield.

"Your mamma might be stressed, but you're having a great couple of days, aren't you? Just an endless string of people you adore." Though I rolled my eyes at him, it was just for show. I loved how happy Watson was in Estes, despite his unrequested role of being the bookshop's mascot and therefore getting petted by strangers much more than he would choose if left to his own devices.

His eyes, wild with excitement, rolled my way, then back as they refocused on the tall silhouette in the tollbooth as we pulled up. Before I had the chance to come to a complete stop, Watson threw himself across my lap and shoved his nose through the crack in the window as I lowered it.

"Well, Watson Charles Page, when did you learn to drive?" Leo leaned out of the tollbooth window, and the two of them met in the space between, Leo's hands stirring up a cloud of fur and Watson whimpering, licking, and trembling all over.

The easy use of Watson's full name threw me off, and I used Leo's distraction to inspect him for a moment, thinking of what Katie had declared about Leo's feelings for me. I knew he adored Watson, but the fact that he remembered I'd given Watson my father's name, Charles, seemed a good bit of confirmation. I must've mentioned it in passing, though I didn't recall. But Leo had held on to the detail.

"What brings you two out?" Still lavishing attention on Watson, Leo glanced my way, his gaze hopeful. "Do you have news? Find something?"

Wishing I could've rewarded that optimism, I shook my head. "Just the opposite, sorry to say. I thought I'd talk to you in person if you have a few minutes."

Sure enough, his expression fell but didn't become unfriendly, and with the final scratch on Watson's cheek, he smiled, then motioned across the row of tollbooths toward the wide meadow at the base of the mountain. "My shift ends in ten minutes, and there's been nobody but those guys for the past few hours. Tourist season is officially over."

"The same is true at the bookshop. There wasn't..." My words trailed away as I followed his gesture. Though I'd grown up visiting Estes Park as a kid to spend time with my grandparents and extended family, and even after living in the town for a year, Estes Park still stole my breath away. Either end of the snowy meadow was filled with two clearly distinct herds of elk, each with massive bulls with crowns of antlers the king would be jealous over, guarding his large harem. And in the middle, a group of twenty or thirty bighorn sheep. So different from the life I'd lived in Kansas City. It was no wonder Leo was so passionate about the animals, or Nadiya for that matter.

Despite being held captive by the beauty, I sensed Leo's gaze on me and looked over to find that his smile had transitioned to something soft and wist-ful. "Spectacular, right?"

"Yeah, it really is."

That time he motioned in the other direction toward the ranger station, which was an actual log cabin that sat a little ways back from the tollbooths. "Meet you over there?"

"You bet." Watson didn't leave my lap until I pulled away from the tollbooth and Leo was no longer beside the window. As if offended, he whirled, bumping the steering wheel, and then leaped to the passenger seat. Once parked, I snapped Watson's leash onto his collar, and we exited the car. Though there were only a few yards to walk to the cabin, because of the risk of mountain lions, I'd learned not to take chances without a leash, unless we were in the middle of downtown. Although, mountain lions had been known to wander along Elkhorn Avenue from time to time as well.

Leo held open the door to the ranger station for Watson and me, and we entered. It was a small main room made up of a table and couch on one side and a computer desk in front of a large picture window looking out over the park entrance on the other. When I'd been in before, Leo had sat at the computer researching an owl feather I'd brought in.

This time he motioned toward the sofa. As we sat, it gave a warning squeak. "Excuse the accommodations. We don't exactly have the budget to turn this place into the Ritz or anything." Leo's smile seemed forced, and he clutched his hands together as he propped his elbows on his knees.

I decided to dive right in. "The couch is fine. I don't want to take too much of your time. I don't know what your plans are. I just thought I'd talk to you in person. See if you could give me some sort of lead, because everything I'm finding, Leo, only makes Nadiya seem more and more guilty."

"She isn't." He flinched, as if his biting tone surprised him as much as it had me. He instantly shook his head and apologized. "I'm sorry. I know it's not your fault. None of this is. And I'm not upset with you. If anything, I'm upset with myself. I've been trying to think of something, but I have no idea where to begin. But no matter what you found, she's innocent."

I believed Katie was right in what she said Leo felt for me, though I'd shoved the obvious away for a plethora of reasons, but with his defense of Nadiya, I was willing to bet I wasn't the only one he held feelings for. "Are you sure, Leo? Sometimes people have a whole separate life than what they present. I don't want you to be hurt at the end of this."

Though he tightened his lips, he didn't snap again. "I am sure. She's become a good friend, Fred. Beyond that, I just have that gut feeling, like the one you describe sometimes. I simply know, with everything in me, that she didn't do this."

"Okay then." I wasn't sure what else to say.

"You don't... have that feeling?" Again his tone took on that hopeful quality.

And again, I had to kill it. I shook my head. "No. I don't." As his shoulders slumped, I rushed ahead, for all the good it would do. "But I don't have a gut sense that she is guilty either." I left out what logic was telling me.

"That's something, I suppose."

Watson had been sniffing around the corners of the room and came over to plop between Leo's feet. Automatically, Leo began stroking him.

Maybe the distraction of Watson would help as I laid out what I'd discovered so far. "I did quite a bit of research on Nadiya this morning. Do you want me to tell you what I found out, or since she's your friend, do you feel like that would be violating her privacy or something if you knew?"

"She's in jail for murder. I doubt she's too

worried about privacy." His lips curved into a bit of a sneer before slipping away again. "Not that I can ask her, since the police still won't let me see her."

I imagined he'd been calling nonstop all day, probably hoping to wear them down, just like he'd hoped to convince them about the poaching. I started to suggest giving them some space, but then decided it wasn't my place to do so, and clearly I wasn't doing such a great job of navigating the police either. I let it pass and focused on why I'd come. "Okay, then, here it is. From what I found online, Nadiya is a member of several animal-rights groups and—"

"So am I! That doesn't mean—" Leo's voice rose, not in aggression, just in self-defense.

"Hold on." I held up a hand. "I'm not accusing you, and I'm not saying that animal-rights activism is wrong."

"I know. Sorry." He took a deep breath and let it out with a sigh. "Please continue. I'll remember that you're just the messenger and you're doing me a favor, doing Nadiya a favor. You can't help what you find out."

"I'm not so sure, especially at this point, whether I'd say I'm doing Nadiya any favors. From everything I've found, I'd call it a pretty open-and-shut case. At this point, I'm only looking into it for you. Because your gut tells you she's innocent." When he nodded, I continued. "Like I was saying, some of those animal-rights groups are the run-of-the-mill kind of organization, but others are fairly extremist. Even so, that in and of itself may not be that big of a deal, but it's a substantial puzzle piece. She's also a master marksman—I found photos with her holding first-place ribbons from shooting competitions. And there's nothing wrong with that, either. I'm not saying there is." I felt the need to say it all as quickly as possible. Leo's brows rose, but he didn't interrupt. "Just because she knows how to shoot and owns a gun doesn't mean she's a murderer. But it does fit with them finding her with the gun in the truck, and she would have the skill to shoot Max in the manner in which he was killed."

Leo looked like he was about to argue again, so I paused. After a moment he simply nodded.

I leaned forward, lowering my voice as if I was breaking bad news. Which, I suppose I was. I figured there was a good chance Leo had already known about the other details if he was as good a friend with Nadiya as he'd said, but she might not have shared the darker details of her past. "There have been no convictions, from what I can find, but Nadiya has had a few charges brought against her, including assault." I paused to judge his reaction, but he didn't give any. "Again, she wasn't convicted, but it seems to indicate that she has a propensity toward violence."

Leo only sighed again, gave Watson a final scratch on the head, and leaned back, sinking into the broken-down sofa.

I studied him, surprised. "You already knew all of this, didn't you?"

He nodded.

I wasn't sure if I'd ever been irritated with Leo before, but I was in that moment. "Then why didn't you tell me? That took me a few hours on the computer today. Not that I wouldn't have looked into it anyway, but if you know things, you need to be upfront with me."

He winced, looking abashed. "Sorry, again. I wasn't trying to hide it from you. I just wanted you to go into it with an unbiased opinion. Although I suppose that's stupid as I knew you'd find all that easily enough." Another wince. "I guess I was afraid if you knew, you'd say it was a waste of time. And it's not. Even with all that you just shared, I know that she's innocent."

Though my irritation didn't vanish, it hurt a bit to know that Leo would think I'd turn him down for any reason. "I don't know if it's going to be a waste of time or not. It sure looks like it, but if you're convinced, that's all I need. Katie too. You know we'll keep looking until we find something that either clears her name or..."

"Makes me accept that she did it?" He looked at me with a cocked brow.

I just nodded.

"Fair enough." He smiled and sounded a little more like his normal self. "I think that's all I know. Have you found anything else?"

I started to say *no*, but then changed my mind. "Do you follow Nadiya on social media? Like Facebook, Twitter, and such?"

He shrugged. "We're friends on there, but as you know, I don't spend much time on any of that junk."

"Okay then, tell me if you're aware of some of the feelings she expresses here." I pulled out my cell and tapped a couple of the social media icons, went to her profiles, and then handed the phone to Leo.

He took a few minutes, tapping back and forth between the various screens and scrolling to read her posts from the past. From the color draining from his face, I knew the answer before he finally spoke. "I haven't seen these. And—" He cleared his throat "—while Nadiya is very passionate, *very*, when we talk about it, she's never actually said things such as this about people meeting the same end as poached animals and such." He tapped a few more times, then shook his head before returning the phone. "But... that's kind of real-life, right? People say things online, drastic things, that they would never say out loud."

"That's true. But I think a lot of people would argue that the things people put on social media, even the ones they wouldn't say out loud, reveal how they truly feel, what's in their hearts and souls." I put the phone away and softened my voice once more. "The thing I didn't find on social media was any connection to her family. Delilah mentioned that the Pink Panthers were the only family Nadiya has."

"That's basically true." Leo nodded openly. "She's estranged from her family."

I considered. "To the point that they wouldn't even come to town when she's been arrested?"

"I doubt they know. Nadiya wouldn't want them contacted." He shook his head sadly. "Sorry, Fred. I know where you're going to go next, but it's not my story to tell. It's Nadiya's."

"It might help her. You said yourself privacy isn't a concern given the circumstance."

From Leo's expression it was clear he was debating, and for a couple seconds I thought he was going to break. He didn't and shook his head again. "Sorry. It wouldn't help, and if you knew her story, I know you, of all people, would sympathize and have her back."

Clearly arguing was pointless. I'd just have to trust that Leo knew what he was talking about. Leo and Delilah. Instead, I moved on to another issue that had been bothering me. "The thing that makes the least sense about this whole thing, regardless of how Nadiya feels about poaching, guns, and all of that, is the timing."

Leo's eyes grew hopeful once more.

"Hardly any time passed between the Cozy Corgi being broken into and Max's murder. How did that happen? And how would Nadiya know that he was a poacher?"

He groaned and his face fell once more. "That's easy. Nadiya listens to police scanners. She would've heard when dispatch communicated the break-in. If one of the police mentioned the suspects name and description and connected him to the sheep, then..." He finished with a shrug.

Good grief, everything pointed to Nadiya Hameed. *Everything*. "Leo, this is looking pretty cut-and-dried."

Somehow his large, muscled frame seemed to shrink, trying to disappear in the sunken couch cushions. "I can't accept that she would do this, Fred. I'm not wrong about her."

I only considered for a moment. "Okay. We'll keep looking." Another thought had hit me driving up to the national park, one that I was surprised hadn't occurred to Katie and me as we'd gone over the things we'd found about Nadiya. "I was wondering... I haven't researched how strict guidelines are being a park ranger, but I'm a little surprised with her past that she got a position, especially here. I know Rocky Mountain Park is one of the most coveted spots. Maybe since she hasn't been convicted, her potential legal trouble wasn't considered?"

He gave me a sheepish expression. "One of the higher-ups in the National Park Service is a good friend of hers. He pulled some strings."

Another hit! "Oh, Leo." I mimicked his expression and sank back into the couch. "This doesn't look good."

Leo just nodded.

Giving up on receiving attention, Watson wandered off, sniffing around the edges of the cabin again, and finally settling in to watch a chipmunk peering at him from the windowsill.

We sat in silence for quite a while, heaviness settling between us.

After a bit, I realized Leo was staring at a small row of lockers on the far side of the room. "What are you thinking?"

"I'm thinking I can't talk to Nadiya, can't get her side of things, so maybe we use her stuff, see if any of it will speak for her." As Leo spoke, he stood and walked toward the lockers. "Maybe we'll find something, who knows what, that might clear her name. We could check here and maybe her apartment."

That seemed like a long shot to me. If anything, that was the opposite of how it worked. You searched for hidden things to prove someone was guilty, or to find clues on what they were hiding, not prove their innocence. But I didn't have any other suggestions, and I couldn't bear to take more hope away from Leo. "You have a key to her locker?" I got up and crossed the room.

Watson left the chipmunk to its own devices and followed me.

Leo gave another sheepish expression, though this was accompanied by grin. "I know how to pick a lock, Fred."

"You do?" That didn't match my version of the Leo Lopez I knew.

He gave a nod and then turned back to the locker and got to work, offering no further explanation.

"*Should* you pick a lock?" My words echoed back to me from the night before, telling Branson I'd never broken the law.

He chuckled as he tinkered. "Don't act like you haven't snuck into places where you weren't supposed to be."

He had a point. Though, each of those times I'd walked the line of the law, if not the letter. Until now.

In less than a minute, the lock clicked, and we opened the rusty metal door with a squeak. Leo took a deep breath, as if he was getting ready to dive underwater, and began to sift through Nadiya's things.

There was nothing. At least nothing of interest. It was a jacket, a couple of scarves, gloves, a flashlight, a few snack items, and an extra pair of shoes, but nothing that proclaimed innocence or guilt.

"I guess that was a waste of time as well." Leo sighed and started to put the boots back but froze when the metal floorboard shifted under the weight of the boots. He leaned forward, inspecting. "I think there's something under here." That spark of hope sounded again.

I stepped nearer, looking over his shoulder as he pulled the thin piece of metal up. "I take it yours doesn't have a hidden compartment?"

"I don't know if it's so much of a hidden compartment as simply a loose bottom. With as old as everything is, I imagine if I lifted up mine, I'd be able to put something underneath it as well. I just never thought of—" He'd been moving slowly, clearly being careful not to cut himself on the rusty metal, but then he froze.

There, underneath the bottom portion of the locker, lying on the dusty hardwood floor, lay a gun.

We both stared at it, and for the billionth time that day, as far as Nadiya was concerned, my heart sank again. "Good grief, how many guns does she have?"

"This doesn't mean..." Leo shook his head. When he spoke again, it was clear he was trying to convince himself as much as me. "It's just a gun, and nothing we didn't already know. The poacher was shot. Nadiya owns guns, legally I'm sure, since she's a master marksman. We... *already* knew she owned guns."

"But we didn't know she was hiding them in

random places." I hadn't meant to say that out loud, and I rushed ahead, trying to fix it, not that it helped. "This doesn't prove she did anything wrong. Obviously she didn't shoot him with this gun. Even if it's illegal for her to have a gun *here,* the police already found the murder weapon in the cab of her truck with her." No... that didn't help at all.

There was a slam of a car door, which caused Watson to yelp and Leo and me both to flinch. Straightening, I looked out one of the windows and saw an older woman walking away from a run-down pickup truck.

Leo stood, then let out a curse. "Etta, crap!" He dropped to his knees and started shoving everything back into Nadiya's locker as fast as he could. "She's not on the schedule till tomorrow."

Katie and I had heard about Etta Squire many times over the months during our frequent dinners at Habanero's. She was another park ranger and liked to claim she'd been on staff since the mountains themselves were formed. Leo often said she was as lazy as a bear hibernating and as grumpy as a grizzly who'd just lost his dinner. It said a lot about the woman as Leo wasn't one to complain about people.

He'd just managed to click the lock back into

place and practically flung himself across the room when Etta opened the door.

"What are you still doing here, Leo? I thought you were off twenty minutes ago. You know I'm not going to approve overtime if..." Her bloodshot eyes widened when she saw me, then narrowed as her gaze flicked to Watson. "Oh. You two." She didn't bother with introductions, though. Apparently she knew who Watson and I were and clearly wasn't pleased by our presence.

"I'm not trying to get overtime, Etta. Fred and I were just... talking." Though Leo managed to make his voice sound completely normal at being caught breaking into Nadiya's locker, the same couldn't be said for the flush that rose to his cheeks.

"This isn't a—" Etta cut off her own words with a long, painful-sounding smokers cough and then sucked in a wheezing breath before refocusing on Leo. "This is a ranger station, *Mr. Lopez*, not a brothel. You need to keep your girlfriend elsewhere." She sneered down at Watson. "And her dog."

Watson didn't growl but once more made me believe he understood a great deal of what was said as he plopped down in front of her and lifted his muzzle defiantly.

If Leo had been red-faced before, it was nothing

compared to the crimson that stained his cheeks then. "Fred's not my... we're not... Why are you here?"

"My fool sister is sick and needed me to pick up kibble for her nasty mutt. So I thought while I was out, I'd..." I could swear a blush rose to Etta's weathered cheeks as she motioned out the window toward the large bag of dog food in the back of her truck and then toward the computer. "That's not your business, boy." She finished with a snap in her tone. "Are you done here? I'm not approving overtime, and I need my privacy."

"Sure, Etta." Leo crossed to the computer desk and picked up our jackets, which we'd discarded over the chair. "We'll get out of your way. Have a good night. See you tomorrow."

Etta mumbled something low on the enthusiasm level, sneezed, and then began to hack again.

Despite the depression I thought Leo was slipping into about Nadiya when we'd found the gun, his eyes twinkled as he whispered to me after we closed the door. "Etta doesn't have a computer at her house, so she comes here to answer messages on her dating site."

I nearly choked and glanced back at the door as if

I could see her through it, then goggled at Leo. "*Dating* site?"

He chuckled. "She doesn't think we know. But we know." His grin faded as his tone turned serious. "Don't give up yet, okay?"

For half a heartbeat, I nearly argued, told Leo that it might serve him better if he could start to come to terms with how things were. But I knew how I would be if I was convinced of someone's innocence when no one else was. I'd turn over every stone, multiple times if I had to, until I either cleared their name or found something to irrevocably prove I'd been wrong. "I won't. How about I call Katie, and the three of us can spend another night on the computer and brainstorming. Maybe we'll hit on an idea that will help me start fresh tomorrow."

TWELVE

The following morning brought Watson even more happiness, to such an extent that Carl Hanson noticed the change in my cantankerous pup as he waddled across Cabin and Hearth—the large all-natural dog bone treat Anna had just given him clutched in his smiling maw. "He was grinning when he came in here. Did you notice, Anna?"

She nodded, staring at Watson's retreating fluffy backside. "I did. He was practically chipper." When he finally squeezed beneath a log four-poster bed and out of sight, she looked at me with suspicion. "Did you put him on one of those doggy antidepressants? It's not natural seeing him quite so giddy."

I agreed. "No. I didn't. He's just had an abundance of people he loves lately. For the second night in a row, Leo and Katie came over for dinner and hung out. Between seeing Barry a couple of days ago, constantly getting to be with Ben in the bookshop, and a sudden abundance of Leo time, I think Watson believes he's in heaven." I barely caught my mistake in time. "And seeing you two so much, of course. Halloween night and now... today."

Anna's smile had just started to falter but slid back into place. I figured she knew, deep down, that Watson used her for treats, but whatever delusion made them both happy, I was good with. Still, the concerned look didn't leave her expression. "That's nice, but I do think I prefer him a little grumpy. Something about it makes him more charming."

"You're just saying that because then he matches your disposition more." Carl's eyes went wide, and his mouth fell open after he finished his statement.

It was all I could do to keep from laughing. Clearly, he'd experienced one of the most challenging aspects of my own personality—thinking some thought in your head but accidentally blurting it out in the open.

Instinctively, Carl sidestepped, clearly expecting one of Anna's frequent swats.

To both of our surprises, she merely cast him a glare, dusted off her gingham skirt as if brushing away the insult, and turned to me. "You're here because of that Nadiya girl, aren't you? Trying to clear her name."

I'd long ago quit pretending I didn't come into Cabin and Hearth to take advantage of Anna and Carl's skill at gossip. "I know she's relatively new in town, but I thought maybe the two of you would have some insight."

With a tilt of her chin, Anna took a deep breath, which showcased her ample bosoms, and nodded decisively. "She is guilty as sin, *that* I can promise you. And I use that word intentionally."

I was a little taken aback. "Really? I thought you'd have a whole range of possibilities."

"Why would I, when it's as obvious as the pimple on Carl's nose? Guilty, guilty, guilty." She dusted her hands off and relaxed somewhat, as if the case were closed.

For his part, Carl ducked his head as his cheeks went scarlet. He did have a rather unfortunate large spot of acne right at the tip of his round nose. He grumbled something, but I couldn't catch it.

It seemed Anna did, as she cast him a glare. "Don't you disagree with me, Carl Hanson. You're just taken in by her wily ways." Anna looked back and forth between the two of us now. "Anyone hanging out with that Delilah woman is guilty, you can mark my word. Running around town in those horrid pink jackets, flaunting their... wares." She reached out, finally swatting Carl's arm, having to lean over to reach. "You can't take a man's opinion on the matter. They're weak when it comes to such issues." Another swat.

Though rather abrasive, I typically found their bickering rather charming and humorous. At the moment, I was beginning to feel sorry for Carl. "I know Delilah has a... reputation, and so maybe her friends get some of that by default, but I hardly think that is akin to murder."

Anna shook her finger at me. Despite myself, I flinched, expecting to get swatted next. "Besides, it's silly you're trying to help her anyway. You decided Branson wasn't good enough for you. Clearly Nadiya has her sights on your park ranger. The two have been seen all over town together. If you lose that handsome man, what other prospect do you have?"

"Anna!" Carl hissed in admonition before taking another step away.

I appreciated the gesture and gave Anna a glare of my own. "I did *not* decide Branson wasn't good enough for me. That's never been the issue. I'm tired of people saying that. We're just not a good..." I shook my head. "I'm not explaining this. It's no one's business. And as far as Leo's concerned, he and I are just friends. And I don't think I'm too good for him either. It's just..." I fluttered my hands in the air, frustrated with myself. "Good grief, that's no one's business either. And I don't need any *prospects*. That's not why I'm in Estes. I wasn't looking for a husband. I came to open a bookshop."

When Anna reached for my arm, I flinched again, but she wasn't trying to swat me. Instead, she patted soothingly. "Breathe, Fred. I'm sorry. I should have known that was such a touchy subject for a woman your age." Her ministrations became patronizing, though I figured she meant well. "Of course you don't need a man. You're a strong, independent woman, right?"

From across the store, Watson poked his head out from under the bed, probably hearing my raised voice. After a couple of moments of inspection, he disappeared once more. Whether because he decided I was fine, or determined that he wasn't going to get another all-natural dog bone treat anytime soon, I wasn't sure.

I made certain my tone was back under control

before I spoke. I was just so sick of everyone having an opinion about my love life, or lack thereof. Although I should have expected it. When my ex-husband had his affairs, it was amazing to me how many people looked down on me in judgment as if I hadn't done my part in keeping his wandering eye in check. "I actually didn't come here about Nadiya to begin with." My voice still sounded a little tight, so I took another breath before continuing. "I'm looking into the angle of Max and Jim Weasel—they're the poachers, and Max was the dead body." Being the masters of gossip that they were, I was certain they already knew that, but still. "Katie, Leo, and I researched them for hours last night. Even so, we didn't even get close to finding all that was on them. It was hard to know where to begin. They have a rap sheet so long, I think you could unroll it down Elkhorn Avenue and still have paper to spare." Having their last name had been the key. It'd been frustrating to see just how much legal trouble they'd been in and that they'd still been roaming free. "Theft, drug trafficking, assault—you name it, it was there. Well, *except* poaching, strangely."

Anna shook her head and sounded apologetic. "Never met them. Don't know a thing about them." Tentatively, she reached out and patted my arm once more, again an apology, probably for prying into my love life or because she didn't know anything about the Weasel brothers.

Beside her, Carl shook his head in agreement.

That surprised me as well. "Really? From what I overheard when they broke into my shop, it sounded like they had rather long business dealings with Sid and Eddie."

"Eddie?" Anna wrinkled her nose. "I don't recall an Eddie."

Carl opened his mouth to say something, then closed it quickly, his eyes wide once more.

I kept my gaze on him as I answered. "He ran the Green Munchies, the dispensary in Lyons."

"Heavens to Betsy, Fred! Why in the world would we know a scumbag like that?" Anna scoffed. "I'm aware the wacky weed is legal across the state now, but I don't approve. I'm just glad we live in a town that doesn't allow it to be sold."

From Carl's pained silence, I was willing to bet he felt differently and had probably partaken in either Sid's or Eddie's products behind Anna's back.

Anna didn't notice, and she continued, "As far as Sid is concerned, he mostly stayed in that nasty little taxidermy shop of his and kept to himself. I can promise you, we didn't run in the same circles." She smiled sweetly at me. "You're a blessing, Winifred Page. You transformed that horrible place into the most charming bookshop in the entire world. It was depressing having to look across the street and see dead animals in the windows of Heads and Tails. Just revolting. Now, thanks to you, and Katie of course"—her gaze flicked toward the four-poster—"and wonderful Watson, it's a delight to be located across from you."

"Thank you." To my surprise, I remembered enough social graces to return the compliment. "And I feel the same. Your store is absolutely lovely."

Anna preened. "*And*, we help you solve murders."

I couldn't help but laugh. "Yes. There's that too."

There was a chime as someone entered behind us, but Anna kept going. "*Exactly*. So take my word for it—this time, there's nothing for you to solve. That woman is guilty."

"What woman?" Paulie stepped up beside me.

I jumped a little in surprise, then pulled him into a quick hug. "Paulie, hi! How are you? I was planning on coming into Paws after I left here. How's Flotsam?"

I could see the answer all over his face as we parted. His eyes were even more bloodshot and swollen than the day before. He looked as if he hadn't stopped crying since I'd seen him last. He just shook his head. "Not good. Flotsam's still..." His voice trembled and faded.

"Still at the vet?" Carl took on a sympathetic tone and rubbed Paulie's back.

Paulie nodded.

"It's just a matter of time, that's all." Anna's tone matched her husband's. "You mark my words. That little guy is too crazy to be sick for long. He and that other one will be bouncing around together, getting into mischief, and driving the entire downtown nuts once more. I promise you."

Paulie managed a weak smile. "Thanks." His gaze flickered to me, and he sounded apologetic. "I should've waited. I would've if I'd known you were planning on coming to see me. But I noticed you heading in here. As soon as my customers left, I came over."

"I'm glad you did. Is there something I can do? Do you need me to watch Jetsam or—"

I was interrupted by Watson shoving between Paulie's and my legs. He pressed his forehead against Paulie's shin. Once more, my little hero proved he understood more than people gave him credit for.

Paulie sank to his knees and wrapped his arms around Watson's neck and cried.

Watson didn't pull away or whimper.

Carl leaned down, continuing to rub circles over Paulie's back.

After a couple of uncomfortable minutes, Paulie's sobs lessened, and Watson shot me a *get me out of this* expression.

I touched Paulie's shoulder. "Is there any improvement?"

Paulie shook his head after ruffling Watson's fur a final time and stood. "No. He is..." Paulie's voice broke again, and he cleared his throat with a head-shake. "Sorry. I can't talk about him without breaking."

"It's okay." I wanted to hug him again, try to fix it, but knew that there was no way I could and that a hug would probably cause him to lose control once more. "You said you were coming to see me. Is there something I can do?"

Another headshake. "No. I just know that you're looking into Nadiya, of course. And thought I'd tell you what I... overheard at"—his words became a squeak—"the vets."

"You just take your time, sweet man." Though Anna's voice was still warm and caring, her eyes glistened like she was about to get a delicious tidbit. "You say what you need to say."

Paulie nodded and stared at Watson as he spoke. "While I was there this morning, Susan Green was in the next room, and I heard her and the vet talking."

"Why in the world was Susan at the vet?" It was one of those moments where my thoughts spewed from my mouth.

"Her pet is sick." Paulie looked over at me, startled, as if it should've been obvious.

"Susan has a pet? *Susan Green* takes care of another living creature?" There was no way that could be true.

"Yeah. She has an albino python name Dexter." Paulie's voice cleared somewhat, evidently the distraction helped. "He's a cute little thing."

Ahhh... that made sense. Susan with a snake, one named after a serial killer no less. *That* I could believe.

"Oh... cute." Anna shuddered and nudged him on. "You, ah... said you overheard something."

"Right." Paulie cleared his throat again. "Right. She was talking about Nadiya. Apparently, they had to put her in solitary confinement because she hurt her cellmate."

"What!" Anna's voice rose, not in shock or horror, but confirming that she indeed was experiencing the equivalence of a five-star dessert.

Odd... I wouldn't picture Susan for one to spread official gossip. Maybe not so odd, actually. I'd been almost certain a couple of different times Susan had let slip a few details of the cases I was involved in one way or another. Maybe she despised Nadiya as much as me.

Paulie didn't require any prodding. "I guess there was a mouse in their cell, and her roommate, or whatever, killed it. Nadiya went ballistic."

And again, with context, it made sense from all I'd gathered about Nadiya.

Anna bugged her eyes and gave me a nod, clearly relaying *I told you so.*

Paulie kept going. "I also heard Susan say that since moving here, Nadiya had sent a couple of strongly worded letters to the police department, saying that if they didn't take action against the poaching situation she'd take matters into her own hands."

That also fit the picture that had been forming of Nadiya Hameed.

This was going to devastate Leo.

And it seemed that Branson truly was done

feeding me any information. That surprised me somewhat. Especially considering it supported his position on Estes Park's new ranger.

I could just imagine what Anna would say about *that* thought as well.

Feeling like I was wasting time, after leaving Cabin and Hearth, I led Watson across the street and down the two blocks toward my uncles' antique shop. On the way, I passed the toyshop where old Duncan Diamond was perched precariously on a stepladder as he hung Christmas lights on the inside of the large picture window. Noticing Watson and me, he gave a little wave, nearly fell, caught himself, and then laughed before finishing the wave.

Just as I was considering going in to help him, his son Dolan appeared from somewhere in the back, didn't notice Watson or me, and began scolding his father. By the time we passed, the two had changed places on the stepladder.

The little intrusion into their family moment took away the sensation of wasting time. Percival and Gary were slightly better at gossip than Anna and

Carl, but even if they didn't have any insight or revelations, perhaps that was exactly what I needed. A family moment. Plus, though they'd called a couple of times since the break-in, we kept missing each other.

When Watson and I stepped into Victorian Antlers, I stopped dead in my tracks as Barbra Streisand's version of "I'll Be Home for Christmas" blasted so loudly I was surprised the antique vases weren't shattering. At my feet, Watson whimpered.

Just as I was deciding this was going to count as another time my uncles and I missed each other, Percival emerged from behind a huge armoire placed in the middle of the store. He tossed a string of silver garland over the top as he hollered toward the back. "I'm not saying it's impossible, Barry! I'm saying it will be expensive."

Someone spoke from out of view, but over Barbra, I couldn't make out who it was. Watson's reaction clarified for me as he instantly went on full alert and rushed forward, straining at the end of his leash.

Barry, apparently.

Knowing there was no backing out at that point, I released Watson's leash, and he tore off through the antique shop, hurtling past Percival and taking the corner at such a speed that the leash whipped around and flicked Percival's calves, causing him to let out a high-pitched screech.

"Rats! Gary! Call the exterminator. We've got rats!" Percival shuddered and did a little jig, which as he hadn't released the tinsel, pulled it down on top of him from the armoire. In all his flailing about, he twisted my direction and paused when he saw me, though he didn't lower his hands from the air. His eyes narrowed, and he glanced down at the floor just to be sure. Though Watson was nowhere to be seen, Percival put two and two together. He raised his voice once more. "Never mind! Not rats! Just a furry tub of grumble and attitude." As he headed my way, he finally lowered his hands enough to stretch them out and wrap me in an embrace. "Fred, darling! Lovely to see you as always. I'm so glad you're okay after all the excitement in your world, although I know you're used to it by this point." He released me before planting two air kisses on my cheeks.

"It's good to see you too. I'm sorry it's taken so long..." I realized I was shouting and pointed up toward the speakers on the ceiling. "Kind of loud, isn't it?"

"It's Barbra, darling. She's a diva. She can be as loud as she wants." Percival adjusted the tangle of tinsel around his shoulders like a feather boa before taking my hand to lead me through the shop. His husband, Gary, came into view as he stood behind a computer at the main counter. In front, Barry, in matching tie-dyed T-shirt and yoga pants—both of lime green and neon green—lavished attention on Watson. Despite his claim, when he released my hand, Percival walked over to the stereo behind the counter and lowered the volume.

Gary left his place behind the computer and headed to greet me with another hug as well. "I suppose I have you to thank for finally lowering the volume. I love Barbra, but goodness, lady, get home for Christmas already."

"Hi, sweetheart!" Barry waved at me, but knew better than to leave Watson lacking for attention so soon.

I waved back but still focused on the ringing in my ears. "I just saw the toyshop decorating for Christmas as well. Is the Cozy Corgi behind if we're not stringing up lights and tinsel?"

"No, Fred, it's just—"

"Absolutely," Percival cut off his husband. "It's the holiday *season*! They all blend together."

Well... that was a vote on Katie's perspective, I supposed.

Gary rolled his eyes as he patted my arm. "No. You're not late. Plus, we saw your Thanksgiving decorations when we tried to catch you the other day. Festive *and* inclusive. I quite approve."

I followed him back to the counter, and joined the others as Gary took his spot behind the computer once more. "Despite the volume, I couldn't help over-hearing. *What's* going to be expensive?"

The three of them exchanged hesitant glances.

Though curious, I held up my hands. "Never mind. You're allowed to have your secrets."

Barry lifted one hand from Watson's head to wave me off, but returned it quickly after a nose nudge. "No, you can know. You're good at secrets. At least better at keeping them than these two, so what harm could be done?" Leaving his hands firmly on Watson that time, he nodded toward my uncles.

Percival looked affronted. "We can keep secrets."

"*I*"—Gary leaned slightly around the computer —"can keep secrets. *You* just hold on to them until the time is the most beneficial for you to elicit the biggest reaction."

Percival shook his head, opened his mouth to argue, then paused to consider. "Actually, yes. That's factual."

I chuckled and felt a little warmth sink in despite

the walk in the cold November day. Time with family was most definitely what I needed, answers or no.

Giving in, Barry shifted from his kneeling position to sitting spread out over the floor with Watson between his legs. "It's too hard for my old knees to do that for very long." He grinned up at me. "As far as your question, your uncles are helping me hunt for an anniversary present for your mother."

"We are *attempting*," Percival clarified. "There are no promises of success. There is no map with an X marking the spot on an antique treasure hunt."

I felt a moment of panic, thinking I'd forgotten their anniversary, then remembered we'd just celebrated. "Your anniversary is in September. You're a little late with the gift." I shook my head the second the words left my lips. "No. You're not. You got Mom a trip to Scotland. A cave tour of all the healing crystals." She had been over the moon.

Barry nodded. "This is for *next* year. And this one's going to take some hard work."

"Hard work that *we're* doing." Percival clarified again, "And there are no guarantees." He leveled a stare at Barry before looking at me. "You may not remember, but Mom and Dad's... er... your grandparents' cabin... er... well, your cabin now, I suppose, was broken into when you were a little girl. Mom had a small jewelry box with several pieces of heirloom jewelry that had been handed down through our family."

I hadn't thought about that in years. "I do remember. Mom was really upset." It stuck in my mind because Mom had never been one to cry about material things, but she'd been nearly inconsolable for several days after the call about the break-in. I knew part of it was worry over her parents being robbed, but it had also been about the jewelry.

Barry continued the story from his place on the floor. "Phyllis's favorite piece was her mother's cameo brooch. Well, her great-great-great grandmother's cameo brooch." A wistful smile crossed his face as he traveled back in years. "She wore it at her high school graduation."

My eyes burned with just a hint of tears at Barry's expression, and the gesture. Not for the first time, I was nearly overcome with gratitude that my mother had gotten to experience two such different men who'd loved her so completely.

"We're going to try to find the very one, hoping that it's changed hands a few times, and maybe someone's trying to get rid of it on eBay or through an estate sale. If nothing else, maybe we can find one similar." Though he spoke to me, Gary smiled down in affection at Barry. "It's a very sweet gesture."

"I'll say!" Percival had moved on to pulling more tinsel out of a large box of Christmas decorations. "My sister is a lucky woman, nabbing herself such a romantic. It's been a long time since *I've* gotten such an elaborate declaration of love."

Gary's facial features as they transitioned from affection toward Barry to annoyed frustration at Percival was nearly laughable. "I got you tickets to another one of Cher's farewell tours last year. In New York!"

Percival sniffed. "True. But you didn't spring for the VIP backstage all-access tickets, did you?"

Gary leaned on the counter. "You're not legally allowed backstage at Cher's concerts anymore after the way you behaved during her *Believe* tour."

Another sniff. "True, but it's the thought that counts."

I did laugh then, and though it earned me a narrowed-eyed glare from Percival, Gary and Barry joined in. Even Watson let out a laughter-sounding chuff. Although maybe he was just trying to keep Barry's attention on himself.

For the next fifteen minutes or so, we talked about everything and nothing, a few family stories, talks of a new restaurant opening that my uncles had attended in Denver. How Percival had won the last monthly spades tournament he, Gary, Barry, and my mother played, one he swore up and down he'd achieved without cheating—much to the protests of Barry and Gary.

Finally the conversation turned to all the events surrounding the poaching and the break-in. "I think I'm wasting my time." It felt like a bit of a confession as I announced it. "Leo is so determined that Nadiya is innocent, and I'm afraid he's going to be utterly crushed when it's proven that she's not."

Barry was standing once more, with Watson asleep at his feet as he leaned against the counter. "You really think she killed that poacher? She seemed like such a sweet girl. Though, I only met her a time or two."

"Every single thing I find out about her says that she would be capable of it, yes." Even as I said the words, I felt like I was betraying Leo. "Honestly, if it weren't for how adamant Leo was about her inno-cence, I wouldn't be looking into it anymore. And at this point, I'm not even doing it because of him believing that she's innocent. I'm just doing it because..."

"Because it's Leo." Gary's deep voice was soft and a little too-knowing.

I nodded.

"Well, I think she's fabulous!" Percival declared with the smack of his hands, startling Watson awake. They exchanged glares before Percival refocused. "She's an easy scapegoat. She defies convention and refuses to be what everyone tells her she should be. So what if she takes a stand for what she believes in with poaching and rubs the police the wrong way?" He gestured between Gary and himself. "I've said it before, and I'll say it again. We've had to fight long and hard against the powers that be to gain equality. And I know plenty who said we should sit down, shut up, be respectful, and wait our turn." He shimmied his shoulders. "Not to mention, the woman's gorgeous and not afraid to flaunt it. Believe me, I understand." He laughed in a way that made it a mystery whether he was only partly kidding or not at all. "There's a lot of jealousy around that, especially when a woman like her, and the rest of that Pink Panther posse, have no problem parading it around."

"I don't think she's a suspect in Max's murder because she's beautiful." I winked at him. "But believe me, if anyone knows what it's like to be tortured because of how attractive they are, I know it's you."

Barry nodded as he ran a hand over his head. "It's true. Balding is beautiful." He winked, confirming he was in on the joke.

"I just left Cabin and Hearth, and Paulie came over. He overheard Susan Green talking about the threats Nadiya had made to the police about taking matters into her own hands. She has a couple of different assault charges, and has a fairly hostile social media presence. She's won multiple shooting competitions, and was arrested in a vehicle that had blood in the back of the truck, *and* the murder weapon beside her in the cab. It's hard to set up someone without their knowledge when they're sitting right next to the murder weapon as they drive."

When Gary spoke, his voice was soft once more, but this time more in apology. "She did come in here asking if we sold collectible antique guns." He grimaced. "Which, we don't."

I thrust my hand out toward him. "See! Granted, shopping for guns doesn't make her guilty, but it's one more piece in a very unappealing puzzle."

"What is your gut saying, Fred?" Barry's voice took on a fatherly tone he rarely used with me—I thought more out of respect for my own father than his feelings for me—but that I'd heard him use with the twins. "Your mother always said you inherited your father's gut. That, even when all the evidence points the other way, your gut instinct is always right."

"That's just it, I don't have a gut feeling this time. Not at all." At his words, I realized that had been part of my problem this whole time. Some sense of embarrassment or failure. That some irrational part of me thought I was proving I wasn't as much like my father as everyone, myself included, claimed.

Barry studied me. "You don't have a gut feeling that she's innocent, but do you have a gut feeling that she's guilty?"

I started to nod in affirmation, then hesitated, actually considering. Did I?

After a few moments, I shook my head, using the motion to test the accuracy of what I was about to say. "No. I don't. Not a gut feeling. Logic says that she's guilty. But I don't have a feeling about Nadiya Hameed one way or the other."

Barry nodded as if that settled it. "Well, then, you're not wasting your time. And you're not failing Leo. Though that wouldn't be true even if you had a gut feeling that she was guilty. But you don't. Therefore, you don't know for certain. That's all you're doing—trying to find out for certain."

That was true enough. "Everything I'm finding points to her. Nothing that takes away every shadow of doubt that she is the one who shot him between the eyes and arranged him on Sheep Island, but it's close." Very, very close. "Leo, Katie, and I were doing research into the poachers last night. They had dealings with Sid and also with Eddie at the Green Munchies. So there's got to be a lot of dangerous connections from that angle."

"Eddie was a sweetheart. There's no way he would've been involved in—" Barry's words trailed off as if remembering Eddie's fate, and his eyes widened. "Maybe *that's* your connection. Whoever killed Eddie is the one who killed Max."

"No. Eddie's case was closed. His killer is in jail." I'd had that same thought, but with the case being settled, it was a dead end. "There's still a chance that it's someone in that world, for sure, but I can't find anyone, nobody at all. And without that, there are no more suspects other than Nadiya. She's the only one with any motive I can find. There's no one else that knew Max was around, or that he was the poacher."

"His brother did."

At his words, I turned to look at Percival and

found him practically covered in tinsel as he tried to untangle the strands. His eyes widened at my expression. "What? Didn't you say that the other guy... whatever his name was, the one that broke in with him, was his brother?"

I nodded.

"Well, you said you felt Max was the leader between the two, that he kept threatening the other guy, belittling him? That could be motive."

"Yeah... but..." But what? I cocked my head as I stared at my uncle. "How have I not even considered that possibility?"

He shrugged. "Probably not listening to enough Barbra."

Watson gave a great shake as we entered the Cozy Corgi, flicking snow over the hardwood floor and the bottom portion of my skirt.

"Watson!" I gestured at the closed front door. "I just asked you to do that outside. For crying out loud!"

He peered up at me with his honey-chocolate eyes and gave an expression that brought to mind what I imagined he looked like as a puppy. Heartbreaker, no doubt. He dipped his head, snagged a larger portion of snow on his tongue with a giant lick and then looked up at me again.

I couldn't help but laugh. "You really are in a good mood, aren't you? If you're helping me clean"— I ruffled the fur between his foxlike ears—"you're forgiven."

With that, he trotted a few steps away, scanned

the bookshop, his gaze lingering on his favorite napping spot in the ray of sunshine pouring through the front window, then tore across the shop and sprinted up the steps to the bakery.

Shaking my head at his disappearing backside, I headed to the counter to rip a sheet of paper towels. Either Ben was in the bakery, or Watson was hoping for a snack. Knowing Watson, probably both. After wiping up the snowy mess, I paused to inspect the shop as well. From the angle, I could just make out the glow of the fireplace near the back in the mystery room. And the flickering glow of the second fireplace on the other side of the shop. With all the Thanksgiving decorations and the Ute trappings, the Cozy Corgi was even more charming than usual. Still... it would be even better with Christmas lights strung here and there. Maybe I should give in to Katie and my uncles' insistence that the holidays really did all blend together. Plus, while I'd owned the bookshop last Christmas, it hadn't been opened. The most decorating I'd gotten to do was some homemade cutout snowflakes on the windows.

After removing my jacket and scarf, I opted to walk past the mystery room and the temptation of curling up on the antique sofa to get lost in a novel, and followed Watson upstairs. Sure enough, Watson had found Ben *and* treats.

Nick sat beside his twin on one of the overstuffed sofas Katie had intermingled among the antique tables in the open-concept bakery.

Katie was carrying over a small tray of what looked like a mix of chocolate pound cake and pumpkin gingerbread. She motioned for me to join them when she noticed me. "Nick just got in from finishing up his half day at school, so I figured we needed a snack. You're just in time."

"It's one of the things Watson and I have in common. We always know where the treats are." After all the conversations I'd had across the downtown that morning, I could use a pick-me-up. Salad or hummus or something would probably have been wiser, but I was more than happy to settle for sugar. I started to head behind the counter to make a dirty chai—Katie had attempted to teach me how to use the espresso machine—when I halted at the new decoration that sat on top of the gray-and-white striated marble countertop. A ceramic, cartoon-looking blue narwhal grinned almost psychotically beside the cash register. "Are we going for a nautical theme?"

Katie dropped one of her hands on her hip. "Are

you kidding? That's *Mr. Narwhal*. He's a Christmas decoration."

Deciding to play along, I nodded. "Great. He's adorable. I didn't know putting the title of mister in front of animals suddenly made them a Christmas decoration."

Katie's face grew serious. "He's a character in the movie *Elf*, with Will Ferrell."

That explained it. "I've never seen that movie. I can't say I enjoy the Will Ferrell type of humor in most movies. But the narwhal is cute."

Katie missed a beat and then threw up her hands. "Well, it's been a nice run. Good being friends with you, Fred. I'll miss you and the bakery." She gave an exaggerated wave to the twins. "It's been lovely knowing you, boys. I'm packing up my toys and going home now."

I laughed as I fiddled with the espresso machine. "Someone's dramatic this afternoon."

"I just feel like the world shifted on its axis, and I'm completely off-kilter. I had no idea my best friend had such a deficit in her taste in cinematography. And to have never seen *Elf*." She hurried over to the espresso machine and bumped me out of the way with her hip. "Scoot over. You can't be trusted not to break things. Not with this new knowledge. Next thing you'll be telling me you don't like Adam Sandler movies."

I didn't answer.

Katie paused from her packing of the espresso grounds to give me a look. "You don't like Adam Sandler movies?"

I let my wince be answer enough.

Katie let out a disgusted sound. "Fine. You might want to look away as I make your dirty chai. I'm going to poison you."

After the twins assured Katie that they liked both Will Ferrell and Adam Sandler movies, we settled down to heavenly snacks. I warmed up with the dirty chai as I filled them in on my conversations with Anna and Carl, Delilah, and my uncles.

"That Beaker woman is just horrible." Katie sounded utterly offended as she expertly arranged a portion of chocolate pound cake and pumpkin gingerbread on her fork. "As if it's any of her business who you date. Or don't date. Besides that, like she has any room to talk. Her husband was an absolutely wretched human being." She popped the food into her mouth and considered. "Which, I suppose means that she actually chose well—they were a perfect match."

Chuckling at her cattiness, I swatted at her. "Be nice."

Nick shook his head. "Katie's not wrong. Mr. Beaker was rather wretched. His wife isn't much better."

I'd forgotten for a moment how horribly Mr. Beaker had treated Nick when he worked at the Black Bear Roaster. "Well, either way, that wasn't quite the point of the story."

Some of the playfulness left Katie's voice. "Right. The point was even more circumstantial evidence against Nadiya."

I nodded. "It was. I'm not saying we should give up yet or anything, but I do think we should try to help prepare Leo for the worst-case scenario."

"I was just reading about this guy put in jail for murder." Even though it was just the four of us—five, counting Watson—Nick's voice was still little more than a whisper. "During the murder, they were at Disneyland. The murder happened several states away. He had tickets and pictures and everything to prove that he was on vacation, but they still put him in jail."

"I heard about that," Katie agreed. "But it was Disney World. Not Disneyland."

"Oh, right." Nick pushed a portion of the chocolate pound cake around with the edge of his fork as he spoke. "There was another guy convicted of murder because his DNA was under the fingernails of the murder victim. The police thought it had gotten there when the victim fought back. But the murder suspect was somewhere else entirely at the time. It turned out that there was a DNA transfer, which they didn't even know can happen."

Katie nodded enthusiastically. "Exactly! Fascinating stuff. The suspect touched something"—she shrugged—"like a carton of milk at the grocery store or something. Some of his DNA got left behind. Then soon-to-be murder victim wanders by, picks up that same carton of milk, maybe buys it and takes it home, and the first guy's DNA inadvertently gets transferred onto his hands when he's pouring himself a glass or whatever."

Ben and I exchanged baffled expressions as we darted looks back and forth between Katie and Nick as if we were at a tennis match.

"The opposite is true as well, though," Nick countered. "There was another guy convicted in the 1980s of murder, and it wasn't until twenty-some years later that he was cleared when DNA testing proved that he wasn't the killer."

I grabbed Katie's hand. "Oh my Lord, what have

you done to this poor boy? You've introduced him to the dark, addictive world of getting lost in a Google wormhole, haven't you?"

She merely shrugged and looked smugly pleased with herself. "You can never have too much knowledge."

Ben chuckled and looked so content and relaxed, my heart warmed. I really was building quite the little family in Estes Park.

I lingered on that for a moment and then refocused on the matter at hand. "Knowledge or not, and as fascinating as those anecdotes may be, they don't really help us. They're the exact opposite of what's going on with Nadiya, who was arrested in her own truck, with the murder weapon, and what is safe to assume was the victim's blood in the back."

"Speaking of, I wonder if they've gotten the DNA of that blood back yet. If it matches Max's." Katie slid a careful glance my way. "No contact from Branson at all?"

I shook my head. "Nothing since he came to my house the night after Halloween. If I'm not mistaken, that's the last I'll hear from him unless we run into each other."

"Or you stumble on more dead bodies." She grinned at me.

"Yes. Or that." With my luck, it was only a matter of time. "Speaking of, Percival had a pretty good theory. He wondered about Max's brother, Jim, being the murderer."

Katie had just taken another bite of the pumpkin gingerbread, and the theory made her suck in a breath, causing her to choke. She pounded her chest for a second, grabbed a sip of my dirty chai, and then managed to breathe. "Goodness, sorry about that! However, that actually works with all that Leo, you, and I found out about the Weasel brothers the other night. The only thing they *hadn't* been convicted of was murder." Her brows knitted. "Although, from what we read, and from what you overheard when you were hiding, it sounds like Max was the one more likely to kill."

I started to agree, but Ben spoke before I could. "That might be, but you can only get abused or tormented so long before you snap. Maybe the little brother had reached his limit."

Nick nodded along but didn't say anything.

Not for the first time, an ache rose in me as I studied the brothers. Though Nick continued to open up more and more as he grew more comfortable, there were times when his silence let me know there were many dark shadows in his and Ben's past he wasn't ready to share, maybe never would.

From Katie's expression, I could tell she was feeling something similar, but she pressed on before it got awkward for the twins. "Even if all that is true, it still leads us back to Nadiya being caught driving the truck, sitting next to the murder weapon. It wasn't like she was being carjacked at gunpoint or anything." Her brown gaze flicked at me. "And with what Paulie overheard, even though it's nothing we wouldn't have assumed anyway at this point, I don't really see any sliver of proof that makes us think that Jim is responsible for his brother's murder. But... we keep looking until Leo's convinced, one way or another."

"Agreed." I was about to turn the conversation back to Ethel Beaker and her war against the Pink Panthers, when the door to the bookshop chimed.

Ben started to get up.

"No, no. I'll get it." I stood, leaving a good portion of the pumpkin gingerbread but taking my dirty chai. "You managed the bookshop all morning. I'll pretend I work here for a few minutes." Giving him a wink, I headed toward the stairs and then looked back at Watson. "You are the mascot. Maybe you should make an appearance today as well?"

With a whimper, Watson glanced up and then over at the table as if hoping for crumbs to rain down like a waterfall.

"Fine, Benedict Arnold. I'll be social on my own." With a final glance at the little group that filled my heart with joy, I walked down the steps into the space that did the exact same thing.

For a second, I didn't see who had come in, but then I found him wandering around in the children's book section. "Dr. Sallee! I haven't seen you in the shop in a while."

The vet grinned. "True. Sorry about that. Busy schedule and all." He paused in his pulling out of books from the shelves, looked toward my feet, and then scanned behind me. "Watson doing okay? Where is the little guy?"

I motioned upstairs. "With one of his favorite people in the world, and doubtlessly begging for snacks."

Dr. Sallee chuckled and shook his finger at me, probably only partially in jest. "I'm sure that makes him happy, but he could stand to lose a few pounds."

I patted my waist. "So could his mamma, so I can't say too much."

Dr. Sallee didn't offer comment on that, and true to his normal, he got right to business. "I actually need your help. My niece is turning eleven this weekend, and I'm at a loss on what to get her. All she does is play video games and spend countless hours on all those social media apps. Snaptweet and Instachirp."

"Snapchat, Instagram, and Twitter?" I gave him a wink. "My mother has a massive following on Instagram."

He shuddered. "Yes, those. And your mother is exponentially cooler than me, apparently." He pulled out another book, inspected the back cover. "Anyway, I'm sure the last thing she wants is books, but I'm trying to broaden her horizons. And I'm feeling a little out of my league here."

While mystery novels were my forte, I actually had quite an affection for children and teen literature. "Do you know any other interests she has besides electronics and social media? If not, I do have a couple of books that revolve around a character who is a gamer, and another where a fifth grader discovers that his principal is a spy when he hacks into the school's website."

"No, I'm afraid that would only encourage her addiction." He gave another shudder. "Kendra always has her head in the clouds. She likes anything fanciful—fairies, unicorns, mermaids. Anything with dragons." He snapped his fingers a couple of times. "She doesn't like aliens, though, or stuff to do with space."

"I have just the thing." As always, sharing the love of my favorite books brought a little thrill. I hurried over to a shelf behind Dr. Sallee and pulled out six thin books. "These were some of my favorites when I was younger. I must've read them fifty times." I held the stack of *The Secret of the Unicorn Queen* books out to him. "The series is out of print now, at least in this format, but I have four sets that I found on eBay. They're only slightly used, but I promise you, if she likes unicorns, she'll love these. It's about a girl who gets transported into this land of warrior women who ride unicorns, where she discovers that—"

"Is there anything about iPhones, social media, or how many likes she gets from her followers?" He stared at the stack with narrowed eyes.

"No. Remember, these were some of *my* favorite books when I was a kid. That was before the days of iPhones and social media."

"Perfect." He snapped the books from me. "I'll take them all."

I handed the books back to him in a Cozy Corgi bag after he paid. "You'll have to let me know how she likes them. If they're a hit, I have a couple other series that she might enjoy."

"I'll do that. Thanks, Fred. You're a lifesaver."

He started to head for the door, and I decided to ask what I'd been trying not to. "How's Flotsam?"

Even as he turned to look at me, dread washed over me. I could imagine the pain Paulie was going through. And even thinking about it brought out my own issues around loss and death.

"Flotsam? As in Flotsam and Jetsam? Paulie's dog?"

"Yes." Strange that he had to ask. Those two corgis are about the most unforgettable animals a person could ever meet.

"Good, I suppose." He sounded confused. "Why? Is Flotsam sick?"

"Well, yeah, you—" Before I could finish the thought, I realized something was wrong. "I must be confused. You *don't* have Flotsam under your care right now?"

Dr. Sallee hesitated. "I... don't typically discuss other people's pets with someone not on their treatment plan. No offense, Fred." His brows creased. "*Should* I go speak to Paulie? Are you concerned about Flotsam's welfare?"

"No! No." I waved my hand as if to stop him,

then lowered it to the counter, utterly confused. "I must've misunderstood something. I'm sorry."

He studied me. "Are you sure? I don't mind popping in."

"Like I said, I've misunderstood something. There's so much going on lately that my brain is just spinning."

He nodded, knowingly. "The poacher murder." He *tsked*. "I won't grieve the loss of such a person, but murder is never the right answer. Especially when committed by someone who was such an advocate for animals. She's not going to do them any good behind bars."

"No, she's not." I forced a smile. "Thanks for understanding. And please let me know what Kendra thinks about the books."

FIFTEEN

Dr. Sallee had barely disappeared around the block before I rushed out of the Cozy Corgi. I was halfway across the street before the cold registered against my skin, and I realized I'd not bothered with my scarf or coat. It wasn't until I threw open the front door to Paws and saw Jetsam curled up close to Pearl that I realized I'd left without Watson. I hadn't even gone upstairs to the bakery to tell Katie and the twins I was leaving.

Pearl hopped up hopefully, scurrying to me in search of Watson. Jetsam simply lifted his head, raised an eyebrow, then sank back to the floor.

"Sorry, guys. Watson's not with me today." Stooping to brush my fingertips along both of their heads, I stepped over Jetsam and headed toward the counter. There was no one to be seen, but I could hear voices slightly raised above the soft cacophony of fish bubbles, hamster wheels, and bird squawks.

Before I reached the door that led to the back room, Paulie stepped through and halted, his eyes wide. "Oh, Fred!" He glanced back at the door, as if hoping someone else were there. "I heard someone come in. I was just…" He thumbed over his shoulder as his words fell away.

Though it had only been a couple of hours since I'd seen him, I could've sworn he appeared thinner. He was gaunt and worn. Eyes still bloodshot and swollen. He looked sick. I reached for his shoulder. "What's going on, Paulie? You're not doing okay."

To my surprise, he flinched at my touch. Just slightly, but it was noticeable. His mouth moved wordlessly for a few seconds, and then he seemed to find words. "I'm sorry that I'm not handling Flotsam being sick very well. I admit. I'm a mess." His words took on an unusually defensive tone. "Not everyone can be as strong as you, Fred."

For a second, I felt guilty at his accusation, then swept that emotion away by remembering why I'd hurried over here so quickly to begin with. "That's actually why—"

Athena stepped into the pet shop from the back

room as well. She too looked strained, possibly angry. "Hello, Winifred."

Yes, definitely angry. Her voice was tight and thin. I wondered what I'd done to make her mad, then recalled the raised voices I'd heard. She and Paulie, obviously. Maybe he was the object of her frustration, not me.

"Hi, Athena." I looked back and forth between the two, debating whether I would get more or less from Paulie with Athena present. "How's everything going?"

"Not good. As you know." Again Paulie sounded irritated.

Athena glanced at him in surprise and then looked at me. "I, ah... was planning on calling you. I—"

Paulie shot her a glare, and she caught herself.

When Athena didn't continue, I decided to prompt her. "Did you get more information? Find something about the Weasel brothers?"

As Paulie had done before, her lips moved wordlessly before sound came. "No. I mean, yes. But nothing... just more of the same. An endless litany of petty crimes with a few major ones thrown in for good measure."

She was lying. At least I thought so. Maybe the two of them had been arguing, and she was just off because I'd interrupted. "Anything that would lead you to believe that Jim could murder his brother?"

Athena tilted her head. "Now there's a thought." She sounded like herself again, mostly. She considered for a few moments before continuing. "I can't say that I did. At least not overtly. But there's enough in the Weasel brothers' past to make it a strong possibility. I'd be inclined to believe it if Max had been the one to kill Jim as opposed to the other way around, but"—she shrugged—"maybe."

Paulie brightened. "That *is* a thought! You could be onto something, Fred."

I narrowed my gaze at him. "You sounded pretty convinced earlier that it was Nadiya."

He flushed, and then paled, his gaze darting around the pet shop. "From what I overheard Officer Green telling the vet, that's what I assumed. But it would sure be nice if it was Jim who was guilty instead of Nadiya. It's a good idea."

Strange. I glanced at Jetsam and then back at Paulie, feeling slightly guilty at trying to entrap my friend. "Have you got Flotsam back yet? Any news on how he's doing?"

He just shook his head, and though he still didn't meet my eyes, his filled with tears once more.

Something was definitely going on, with him *and* Athena, but I could tell his tears were real. He was worried sick over Flotsam. Still, I pushed. "How much longer does he have to stay for observation?"

"I'm not sure. They have to—" Paulie's voice caught with emotion and he had to give himself a shake. "I'm not sure."

Athena stepped closer to Paulie and began to rub his back as she had the other day. As she did, she gave me an inquisitive glance.

Time to go in for the kill. "Dr. Sallee was just at the Cozy Corgi. He was looking for a birthday present for his niece."

"He was?" Paulie's brown eyes flashed up, wide and a bit afraid, confirming my suspicions.

"He didn't know anything about Flotsam being sick, Paulie." I took a step forward. Though I kept my voice firm, I tried to put as much tenderness in it as I could.

Athena leaned back, gaping at him. "Paulie?"

"I... I..." Paulie fluttered his hands, once more searching around the pet shop, then flinched as it seemed he discovered what he'd been looking for. "I never said anything about Dr. Sallee. Flotsam isn't at Estes Park Animal Clinic. I never said that either. He's... at a specialist in Denver. He's really, really sick. Worse than what they could handle up here."

Athena darted a look my way, then turned her furrowed browed expression on Paulie. Clearly, whatever was going on with Paulie, she wasn't aware of it.

I took Paulie's shoulder once more, felt him flinch again. "Paulie, you said you overheard Susan talking to Dr. Sallee about Nadiya."

"No. No, I didn't." He shook his head, somewhat frantically. "I said she was talking to the vet. I never specified Dr. Sallee. It was a vet in Denver." He nodded as if to himself and then finished in a whimper, "She was in Denver as well."

The story was so ludicrous that I almost felt sorry for him. I *did* feel sorry for him. "Paulie, why are you lying to me?"

"To us," Athena clarified.

Paulie simply shook his head, tears streaming down his face.

Suddenly I knew. Not specifically, but I knew. "Paulie, look at me." I tightened my grip and waited until his tear-filled and bloodshot eyes rose to mine once more. "You told me before that there were things in Estes that I still didn't know about, that there were things you couldn't tell me."

He gave the most minute of nods.

Beside him, Athena's expression of shock returned. That surprised me a bit. They were so close, I figured he'd told her about our conversation.

I could ponder that later. "You told me that you would tell me if I was ever in danger."

"And I would." Though his voice trembled, there was truth. "If you are in danger, I would tell you." He looked at Athena. "Either of you."

"Paulie, are *you* in danger?"

He shrugged.

I knew the answer before I asked the next question. "Flotsam is in danger, isn't he?"

He froze, and though he didn't answer, didn't nod or shake his head, when he met my gaze again, the answer was evident in his eyes. "Please let this one go, Fred. You're not in danger. I'd tell you if you were. But... by you looking into this, you're putting people in danger, people you love."

"Paulie, if you tell Fred, if you tell us, we can help—"

He cut Athena off with a glare. "No. If I say anything more, then you're both in danger, and this is bigger than Fred can solve. Bigger than anyone can solve." He pulled his shoulder free from my grip and stepped away. "I need you both to leave. Please."

He headed toward the back room, and Athena rushed after him.

I watched them go, feeling slightly dazed, slightly nauseous.

A couple of hours later, I was on my way home with Watson in the passenger side of the Mini Cooper. Katie and Leo were coming over shortly to have another night of brainstorming. I had a feeling it was going to be a *very* late night of brainstorming.

As I turned onto the street that would wind past the very un-Estes Park-like subdivision and then lead back through the forest to my little cabin, I got a call from Athena. "Hey. You all right?"

"Hardly." She sounded exhausted. "I've been debating what to do ever since our conversation with Paulie. He made me promise I wouldn't tell you. Swore it would only make things worse. That it would put you, and possibly me, in danger. But I think it's better to face it head-on."

"I agree. It's always better to face things head-on." A tingle of fear entered, and though it probably showed just how crazy I was, an even bigger rush of excitement. "What is it?"

"It's why I was at Paulie's. As soon as I found it today when I was researching at the paper, I went to him. I planned on going to you next, but... well... you saw."

"I sure did." I wished she'd just blurt it out already. "What did you find?"

"Honestly, I didn't think it was much. Just a strange coincidence or connection. Until Paulie's reaction. Now I think it's much bigger than I feared. Do you remember the name Charles Franklin?"

I hit the brakes, sending Watson flying but managed to shoot my hand out to catch him just in time. He glared, but I didn't have it in me to apologize or try to soothe. My blood turned to ice. "Of course I remember Charles Franklin. Not only did he try to kill Paulie, but he was involved in the case my dad was investigating when he was murdered, remember? He was part of the Irons crime family in Kansas City."

"Oh, of course. I forgot that part. Sorry. There was so much happening when you mentioned it that I..." She paused.

"Don't worry about it." I hated to cut Athena off,

but I needed to know. "What about Charles Franklin?"

"Like I said, it wasn't much. I just found an old article from a paper in Eureka Springs, Arkansas, about a drug bust. There was a list of suspects. Max and Jimmy Weasel were on there, as was Charles Franklin. I don't have anything other than that. Just proof that they knew each other, if the article was correct. I nearly passed it off as a coincidence, but..."

"Even if I believed in coincidences, which I don't, this wouldn't be one of them. Not when Paulie has been lying to us and is clearly terrified." Still, it didn't make any sense. Not at all. "But it's not like Franklin could be here. He was killed in Glen Haven."

"I know." Athena sounded baffled. "You think it's possible that Nadiya is related to him or something? That she came here for revenge?"

"I've seen photos of Charles, he didn't look Pakistani. But maybe he and Nadiya were involved romantically." It was a thought, but I dismissed it quickly. "Unless she went to a whole world of trouble to make a bunch of fake social media accounts over the last several years, I don't think she'd have anything to do with a man who's involved in poaching and animal trafficking." I'd nearly forgotten about Nadiya over the last couple of hours. "I'm not sure what the connection is to all of it yet, but even though I have no idea how it was managed with her in the truck, I'm about willing to bet that Leo was right. Nadiya is innocent."

SIXTEEN

"So let me recap, to make sure I've got it." Leo listed things off on his fingers. "Paulie was lying about his dog this entire time. Flotsam isn't at the vet, never has been. Which means what he claimed to overhear Susan say about Nadiya and her letters to the police wasn't true."

"We now know that the Weasel brothers have a connection to Charles Franklin." Katie jumped in, but as she spoke, Leo still kept track. "Which means two out of those three are dead. Charles and Max."

My skin tingled at the connection to the Irons family and the death of my father. "And all of this confirms, at least seems to, the theory that this is bigger than just poaching." I touched Leo's arm from across my kitchen table before he could object. "That's not downplaying poaching, just that there are a lot more spokes to this wheel. And that it connects to things far larger than simply what's happening in Estes and the national park."

"No, I don't disagree." Leo held the soupspoon in midair. "Poaching often goes along with other high-level, and often deadly, crimes. But I'm still having a hard time accepting that Nadiya was part of it."

"I don't think she was." For the first time since Max's murder, my gut seemed to wake up at my declaration. I repeated the statement, testing the resolve. "I don't think she was. If Nadiya was connected to the Irons crime family, if that's who's behind all of this, then her legal issues as well as her social media activity doesn't make sense. They would need her to be squeaky clean to fly under the radar if she was acting to help them in some way. On the flip-side, if she was part of them and they were trying to set her up by planting a fake social media trail, she would've caught on unless they adjusted all the social media going back *years* and her record all in one night, which doesn't sit right."

We fell into silence, each of us considering as we ate. Katie had brought over her homemade French onion soup and a new version of the bread with the garlic base, formed into round loaves. Once at the house, she hollowed out the inside of the bread to make bowls, ladled in the French onion soup, and covered each with a thick layer of Gruyere. As we sat down to brainstorm, she presented us with piping hot bowls of perfection covered in bubbling, golden brown cheese.

"I know I say this with everything you make—" I ripped off a part of the bread bowl and used it as a spoon to get a heaping portion of oniony goodness and stringy cheese "—but I think this is my favorite thing you've ever made."

Leo hummed his agreement.

Katie shrugged it off. "With as cold as it is outside, and the heaviness of all we've been dealing with, soup seemed the right way to go." Her eyes twinkled. "But, yes, I think I did find the magic combination for this bread recipe."

I peered down at Watson, who was enjoying his feast at Leo's feet. "It was also super nice of you to bring steak for Watson. Talk about lavish."

She shrugged again. "Well, dogs aren't supposed to have garlic or onions or all that much cheese. Couldn't very well cook for us and leave the Scooby of our Scooby Gang hungry."

Leo chuckled but sounded strained.

"Chief Briggs always puts Paulie as our fourth Scooby Gang member." Though I knew she'd been attempting humor, it made me sad. "I'm really worried about him. He's clearly terrified for Flotsam, and maybe just in general as well."

"So if Flotsam isn't sick and with the vet, where is he?" As if the thought of the missing corgi was too much, Leo bent slightly so he could stroke Watson as he spoke.

"With Charles Franklin is my bet." As soon as the words left my lips, the gut feeling came back once more.

Katie looked at me as if I'd lost my mind. "Sweetie, Charles Franklin is dead."

"I know that." I rolled my eyes though I grinned at her. "I mean Flotsam is with him *figuratively*. Like we've said, there's no coincidence that Charles's name came up again. He tried to kill Paulie, and now Flotsam is gone, and Paulie is worried sick and lying to people that he loves."

Leo sat up straighter, excitement bright in his honey-brown eyes. "Max and Jim are revealed as active poachers and break into the Cozy Corgi looking for marijuana, and they have past ties to Charles Franklin. That may or may not mean they have ties to the Irons family. From what you've said, Fred, though you're not sure to what extent, Charles was involved in your father's death, or at least part of the organization of drug dealers your father was investigating that was also part of the Irons family."

"Exactly." I nodded as I tapped the table. Some of Leo's excitement was contagious, but the sense that this was connected to my father was more surreal than anything else.

Katie spoke, sounding as if she were puzzling it out through her words. "So... Charles Franklin has Flotsam, or at least whoever his group is now, has Flotsam." Still considering, she finished with a large spoonful of soup, a long trail of cheese bridging her lips and the bowl before she pulled it apart.

"Poor Flotsam." Leo nodded as he sobered. "It all kinda makes sense."

"Yeah. It does." My skin tingled.

"What if Chief Briggs has Flotsam?" Leo asked suddenly.

Katie and I both looked up at him.

"Hear me out." He rushed ahead before we could say anything. "Paulie has always been terrified of him."

"That's true, even when Briggs knew Paulie's secrets and was in charge of keeping him safe." My mind began spinning with the possibility. "I saw myself how Briggs bullies him. I didn't think much of it because"—I shrugged—"well, he does that to everyone."

Leo jumped right in, nodding. "The police have never been open to my complaints about poaching. That would make sense if Briggs is involved. If he was somehow the ringleader of it."

"Or maybe Charles Franklin was the ring-leader," I pondered aloud, "and Chief Briggs took him out. I don't know. Either way, for whatever reason, maybe he's the one who killed Max." If Briggs really was involved that could mean Branson knew and was trying to keep me from digging too deep. Maybe he was working undercover, trying to gather evidence. Or... maybe he was in danger. Him and Susan.

"Why would Briggs kill Max?" Again it sounded like Katie was working things out in her own mind as opposed to actually asking questions, but she brought me back to the moment. Trying to figure out where Branson, or Susan for that matter, fit in it all was too much. "Max and Jim didn't seem like much more than incompetent lackeys."

"Maybe too incompetent." Leo let the spoon fall against the bread bowl and left it there as he propped his elbows on the table. "This actually makes sense, or at least more than anything else. If Chief Briggs is behind Max's death, it would've been easy for him to set up Nadiya."

From below us, Watson let out a long, loud, satisfied belch.

Katie smirked, then winced. "If we're right, then that means poor little Flotsam is with Chief Briggs. That's terrifying. I can imagine how he's being treated."

"No wonder Paulie is such a mess." I looked down at Watson, my heart aching. "Briggs looks at dogs as if he wants to squash them like bugs. I'd be beside myself if Watson was with him for more than two minutes."

"You don't think..." Katie stiffened, and when she started again, her voice was barely a whisper. "You don't think he hurt Flotsam? Killed him?"

The thought only had to play out for a couple of seconds before I shook my head. "No. At least I don't think Paulie believes so. If we're right, and it is Briggs, then he's using Flotsam to hold over Paulie's head, making him lie about Nadiya or whatever. Though I can't imagine him putting up with Flotsam for a second longer than he has to."

That time, Leo stiffened and sucked in a gasp.

Katie whirled on him. "What? I know that sound. You just had an idea."

"Hold on." Leo held up a finger as he squinted. "Let me think about this."

Katie and I exchanged glances, then focused on Leo as we waited.

As he thought, Leo shook his head several times and made a few grunting noises. When he finally met our gazes, there was a mix of determination and anger in his expression. "Briggs doesn't have Flotsam. Etta does."

"Who?" The word barely left her lips before Katie shook her head. "Oh! Etta Squire, your cranky old park ranger. That's a random theory."

"Maybe it is, but maybe... not." He considered a few more seconds and then tapped the table with his forefinger.

Watson let out a startled yelp, and Leo dipped his hand to pat Watson's head to soothe him, but kept going.

"She's always downplayed the poaching. Shrugged it off as just being part of the job, how the world works. That the rest of us were young and had on rose-colored glasses and thought we could change the world. She never stood in the way exactly, but... now that I look at it from this angle... close." His brown eyes went to me. "When we were at the station two days ago, I didn't think anything of it, but she was sneezing, and her eyes were bloodshot. She's allergic to dogs. And cats, for that matter. I thought maybe she just had a cold or something, but if she is part of this—"

"If she's part of this, then she could have been helping Chief Briggs from inside the park."

Leo glanced toward Katie at her interruption, then nodded and kept going. "Right. And if she's part of this, maybe she was in charge of taking care of Flotsam, and she's having an allergic reaction."

She had seemed pretty miserable. I'd chalked it up to a smoking habit based on her voice and her cough. A thrill shot through me at another memory. "She had a bag of dog food in the back of her truck, remember? She said it was for her... niece or someone."

A huge grin spread across his face. "Her sister. You're right, Fred. Even more proof."

Again, that feeling in my gut settled. It was relaxing. I hadn't realized how much I'd come to depend on that sensation. "We're on the right track. We may not have the details right, I don't know, but we're getting there. Finally."

"I know where she lives. I could swing by, see if I can hear Flotsam, or wait outside long enough to see if she lets him out to go to the bathroom." Leo started to stand.

Katie shot out her hand, holding him in place. "Hold on. Let's slow down a little bit. If this crazy theory is right, and some sinking part of me thinks it is, we're not just dealing with grumpy old Etta Squire. We're dealing with Briggs, a man we think may have killed or have had at least two people killed. Let's be as sure as we can before we go rushing into anything."

Though he looked like he wanted to argue, Leo sat back down after a few moments. "You're right. Of course, you're right. But how do we figure out if she has Flotsam without going there?"

"I can call Paulie." My heart was thundering away, some exhilarating mix of excitement and fear. "If we're right, and I put it to him point blank, I don't think he'd lie about it. Or if he does, I don't think he'd try very hard to cover it up."

"And if Briggs has his phone tapped or has him under surveillance?" Leo grimaced. "Maybe I'm sounding paranoid, but at this point..."

Katie practically popped up from the table. "Hold on, I'll be right back. She hurried into the living room and came back with her laptop, placed it on the table, and began tapping away before she'd even sat back down. "Let's see if Etta has a Facebook page."

Leo scoffed. "Etta hates people. Why would she have a Facebook page?"

"You said yourself she's pretty heavily involved in online dating."

Katie straightened, looking at Leo as if he was going to contradict my reminder. When he didn't, she swatted his arm. "For crying out loud! How have you left out that detail when you've described her to me?"

He grimaced again. "I try not to think about Etta dating, online or otherwise."

Katie rolled her eyes and turned her attention back to the computer, and almost instantly smiled in triumph. "She does have a profile. Now, we only need a couple more strokes of luck."

It was hard not to ask questions as Katie typed away, but when she was on a roll, it was best to just let her do her thing. After a few more seconds, she nodded and gave a happy shimmy but kept going without explanation. A few more keystrokes, and she fist-pumped the air. "Got her and luck *is* on our side!" She beamed at Leo and me. "Not only is Etta on Facebook, but she's connected to her sister, Sylvia. It seems Sylvia isn't the least bit concerned with online privacy. Under her profile on Facebook she has her address, birth date, employment, and her phone number. She might as well throw in her Social Security number for good measure." Katie leaned back in her chair so she could dig her cell out of the pocket of her jeans.

"What are you going to do?" Leo sounded wary.

She winked at him and she stood. "Just watch. And cross your fingers. We need just a little bit more luck that she's similar to others in her age group and feels weird about letting calls go right to voicemail." She began tapping on her cell. "I'm just going to block my number..."

After a few more seconds, she held the phone to her ear and began to pace around the table. She had the volume up so loud that we could hear the ringing on the other side.

Leo, Watson, and I swiveled in our spots, watching as she slowly circled us.

There was a glitch in her step, and her face brightened. "Hello there. Have I reached the residence of Sylvia Bortz?" She began to pace again. "I have? Wonderful. May I speak to her, please?"

Leo and I gaped at each other. Katie's voice had taken on a British accent. Or, at least what was meant to be one. Leo smirked, and I had to look away to keep from laughing.

"Oh, this is she? Wonderful." Katie's footsteps sped up and Watson scooted under Leo's chair. "I hate to bother you on this fine evening, but I'm with the Charleston Dumb Friends League, and we're doing a survey." There was a protest on the other end of the line. "No, I'm not going to ask for donations. Please don't hang up. I promise it will only take a couple of seconds. We're just doing an... animal... census." There were some more words, but I didn't have time to make them out before Katie rushed on. "Our first question is, how many dogs do you have in your household currently?"

She halted again when the woman answered.

She looked over at us with wide eyes as she spoke to the phone. "Oh really? You don't have any of those disgusting mongrels at your residence you say?"

Something else unintelligible.

"Do you ever have one stay the night?"

The voice on the other line went shrill.

"Because... dogs have sleepovers too." Katie's cheeks turned crimson, and she hurried on as she picked at the fuzzy decal of a snail dueling a salt-shaker embroidered on her sweatshirt. "Well, that marks you out of the running for finishing the survey.

Sorry about that. And thank you for your time."
Katie clicked a button on the phone and shook it in
the air in triumph, her voice returning to its normal
state of being. "No dog! And Sylvia sounds just as
miserable as her sister." She flinched, looked at the
screen of the cell, and then practically sank against
the table. "Oh, thank goodness. For a second I
thought I forgot to hang up."

Laughing, Leo patted her on the shoulder. "Brilliantly done."

Chuckling along, I echoed his sentiments. "Good
job, Katie. I didn't know you could act as well as you
could bake."

"I wouldn't go *that* far." Her eyes narrowed.

"And *I* didn't know you were part British."

Katie flinched as she looked at Leo. "Part British?
I'm not. What made you think that?"

He studied her for a second as if to see if she
was teasing. "You didn't mean to do a British
accent?"

Her mouth fell open. "I *didn't* do a British
accent!" She looked to me. "Did I?"

"You did." I laughed again. "Or at least something British adjacent."

Her cheeks flushed even brighter. "Oh.
That's odd."

"And why the *Charleston* Dumb Friends League?" Leo was still laughing as he beamed at her.

"Did I say Charleston?"

We both nodded.

Katie waved her hands in the air. "I don't know. It's called improv. I was just saying whatever came to my mind."

Tears were streaming down Leo's face as he lost himself in laughter. But he managed to gasp out a few words. "Says the woman who just told us we needed to slow down and that we don't want to go rushing into anything."

She narrowed her eyes at him, and smacked Leo on his shoulder. "Well, I got the job done, didn't I? We now know that Sylvia does not, in fact, have a dog, which means Etta is lying. It lends more credence to our theory."

Laughing as well, I soothed my hand up and down her arm. "You did amazing, Katie. You really did. I wish, however, that I'd recorded that for posterity."

"You're both awful, horrible human beings." She bent to pet Watson. "Except for you." She made her way around the table to plop back into her chair. "I think I want out of the Scooby Gang." Then she too began to chuckle.

Once the laughter died enough, things became serious again. I almost hated to ask the next question. "So what do we do with all this? There's a lot of what-ifs, but I'm not sure who we turn to. If Briggs is involved, it's not like we can call the police." And worry spiked over Branson.

"I think we could." Leo was still wiping tears from his cheeks, but was utterly earnest. "Susan has always been receptive anytime we made a complaint about poaching. I think she'd have our backs."

"Are you insane?" Katie's expression communicated that she clearly thought he was. "Susan might like *you*, but she hates Fred, and me by extension. Whether she's in on it or not, the second we call and report this, she'd run straight to Briggs." Without waiting for a reply, Katie turned to me. "I say we call Branson." She held up a hand before I could protest. "I know things are... awkward between the two of you. But if we can convince him, he'll help."

Leo made a sour face but didn't say anything.

"No. I'm not calling Branson." That time I held up a hand before Katie could protest. "And I'm not just being stubborn. It's not fair for me to keep pulling him into things, especially when were not really certain. With something like this even more so. We're talking about his supervisor. We're not sure what danger we might put him in. Especially if he doesn't believe me and says something to Briggs." Though I didn't pause in my explanation, my brain was rattling on. This would explain many things— why the chief hated me so much, why he demanded Branson shove me out of cases, especially this one. "I don't want to put him in that position, not yet. And I'm not sure about Susan. She and Briggs certainly don't have a good working relationship, but I'm not willing to bet that she hates him more than me. I don't think it's wise to risk finding out."

Though it looked like it took effort, Katie didn't argue. "Fine, then. How do we get more proof?"

"Back to my plan." Leo stood again. "I'll go to Etta's house, hang out, see if I can hear Flotsam or something." He glanced down at Watson. "He can come with me. From the way Flotsam responds to Watson, if they smell each other, I bet Flotsam would start barking inside."

"And again, I ask, are you insane?" Katie yanked him back down into his chair. "If we're right, and Etta is a part of this, and she sees you? And if we're right about Briggs? Then she calls him, he shows up, and you and Watson are the next bodies on Sheep Island."

He glowered but didn't disagree.

Truth be told, I was edging toward Leo's reasoning. Now that it felt like we finally had movement, I wanted answers sooner rather than later. But Katie wasn't wrong.

Maybe a compromise... I leveled my gaze on Leo. "Do you know Etta's work schedule?"

He nodded. "Yeah. She's on tomorrow morning. I'm on tomorrow afternoon."

I looked at Katie. "Then tomorrow. We'll check it out tomorrow."

SEVENTEEN

"And I thought *my* cabin was out in the woods." I stared out the passenger side window of Leo's Jeep as he parked on the gravel driveway of Etta's tiny shamble of a house. It was so far back in the woods, at the end of a long narrow road, there was no sense in parking a distance away and trying to disguise that we were there. The most we'd attempted in terms of disguise was using Leo's Jeep instead of my too-easily recognizable volcanic-orange Mini Cooper.

"I wasn't kidding about her not being a people person." Leo shifted the Jeep into Park, turned off the engine, and unfastened his seat belt. "She wouldn't be getting any unsolicited visitors out here."

"That makes the perfect place to keep Flotsam, then." My heart was pounding so hard I wondered if Leo could hear it. I wasn't sure whether I hoped we'd find Flotsam and have our suspicions confirmed or not. I didn't really want to start back at square one, but the other possibility seemed too large to face.

We'd waited until half an hour after Etta was scheduled to go in for her shift at the park. We also decided it was smarter to have Katie stay behind. Both so she could be with Ben at the Cozy Corgi and keep up appearances and so she would be able to bring in reinforcements, just in case.

Maybe saying *we* decided was a bit of a stretch. Katie pointed out that we could simply put a Closed sign on the Cozy Corgi, claiming that she and I both had food poisoning or something. She also argued that the only thing that could possibly go wrong was Etta herself being sick or finding some other reason to be home and that in such a case it would be better to have three against one as opposed to two against one. I worried that she wasn't going to forgive me for putting it to a vote.

I shoved that worry aside as I snapped on Watson's leash and we exited the jeep. It was the right decision, the smart decision. Plus, we needed to focus.

Leo inspected what remained of the crusty snow around Etta's house. "There are the tire tracks from her truck and footprints from it to the door, but I don't see any evidence of Flotsam anywhere."

"No, me neither." We'd come up with the semblance of a plan on the drive over, so Leo and I didn't have to discuss anything. We walked up to the front porch, and he knocked on the door. Since the truck wasn't there, we knew Etta wasn't home, but still, just in case.

No one answered.

Following our plan, we left the porch and began to walk around the house, checking for any signs of Flotsam. We both swore we weren't going to break in unless we found some evidence that he was there. I wasn't entirely sure either one of us planned on sticking to it, but we were going with the pretense anyway.

Watson sniffed along the ground curiously, weaving back and forth from the foundation of the house to the edge of the trees that surrounded the property only a couple of feet away—much like he did on our walks to the forest around my cabin. When we turned the corner to the back of Etta's house, Watson whimpered, seemed to catch a scent, and hurried forward.

"Leo, I think—"

"Yeah, I see." Leo hurried along beside us as Watson beelined to the back door, shoved his nose against the jamb, and then looked back at me with a bark.

"Do you smell Flotsam, buddy?"

He whimpered and barked again, clearly answering my question.

"That's enough answer for me."

"For me too, but if it wasn't..." Leo leaned his hand against the side of the cabin and lifted one of his feet. "Here's more proof."

I looked down to see that he'd stepped in something, and then noticed that same something in a few different spots around us. I pointed to a small patch of snow a few feet away. "And there's even more proof, as if we needed any."

Leo glanced at the corgi-sized pawprint in the dirty patch of snow, then met my gaze. "Between Watson, the poop, and that, I'm convinced Flotsam is here. Although I'm not sure why we don't hear him barking, so maybe *was here* is the correct phrase. But it's enough reason for me to think we were right. Are you sure you want to go through with this?"

I didn't even have to consider. "A hundred percent."

"Are you sure? Up until this point, you haven't actually broken any laws when you've been looking into the murders. Breaking and entering is definitely a—"

"Shut up, Leo." I gave him a wink and laughed, sounding fuller of bravado than I actually felt. "Besides, technically we broke that with Nadiya's locker, so put your lock-picking skills back to work."

He grinned but didn't argue anymore and focused on the doorknob.

Watson continued sniffing around the base of the door, whimpering, clawing at it every once in a while, like he was trying to dig beneath.

After only slightly longer than it had taken Leo at the locker, there was a click and with a satisfied nod, Leo turned the handle and opened the door.

No sooner had we stepped in than I heard the sound of claws, similar to what Watson had just been doing trying to get in.

Watson took off so fast that he jerked the leash from my hands as he tore through the small house. After a second, he barked.

Leo and I entered a decent-sized living room. I could see the front door on the other side, but the curtains were drawn and things were dim. Through the doorway on the right, there was a small kitchen. On the left, where Watson had disappeared, was a hallway. Leo and I followed and found Watson whimpering and clawing at another door.

Neither of us spoke, and just as my hand reached the doorknob I heard whimpering from the other side. "He's in there." The *why* he wasn't barking scared me to death. I tested the doorknob gently to see if it was locked, but it twisted easily enough that I pushed open the door.

Flotsam barreled through, crashing into Watson in a storm of whimpers and batting paws and wagging of nubbed tails.

For his part, Watson desperately licked Flotsam all over, as if he was a long-lost friend. Which, I suppose he was.

As I knelt, Flotsam's attention turned to me, and I reached for the tricolored corgi's head. "Oh, poor baby." He had on a muzzle, the cage so tight that he didn't have enough room to bark, though it didn't seem tight enough that it was causing him any pain. With a couple of quick snaps, I unleashed the muzzle at the back of his head and pulled it off.

Flotsam let out a bark and began completely bathing my face in corgi kisses. For the first time in our acquaintance, I didn't try to get him to stop and was a little surprised when I realized a couple of tears had escaped.

Leo knelt beside us, ruffling Flotsam's and Watson's fur and receiving his own wash of doggy kisses. "We're glad you're okay, you crazy thing."

Watson pranced about, proving that he was nearly as thrilled as Flotsam.

Leo looked at me over the bouncing dogs. "What do you think? Stick to the plan or take Flotsam and get out of here?"

Part of me must've thought we'd been wrong. That we wouldn't actually find Flotsam in Etta's cabin, because now that we had, I wanted to take him and run. But all that would accomplish was prove Etta's involvement. We needed to try to find some kind of proof of who she was working with. If we were right that Chief Briggs was part of this but didn't find proof, it would be easy enough for him to simply blame her. Unless Paulie would be brave enough, with Flotsam safe and sound, to say all that he knew. I didn't want to depend on that, though. "Stick to the plan. Where should we start?"

"Luckily, there's not much to look through." He glanced around, then gave a shrug. "I'm betting the bedroom. Something in a drawer. Although I'm not really certain what we'll find. It's not like she and Briggs are going to have some sort of formal contract."

The dogs' barking increased in their celebration.

"True, but there might be something. We'll know it if we see it." I reached out to stroke Watson. "All right, buddy, I know you're happy, but try to breathe. You'll call in the neighbors, even though there aren't any." As I spoke, I realized from the way he was glaring over my shoulder that I'd misinterpreted Watson's barking.

Leo and I followed his gaze at exactly the same moment, just as there was a click of the rifle that was aimed at us.

"Turns out it was a good day to forget my lunch." Etta sneered over the barrel of the gun, her eyes even more bloodshot than when I'd seen her last time.

Growling with a fury I wouldn't have thought possible of Flotsam, he rushed at her, fangs bared.

Just before he was out of reach, I managed to snag his collar and pull him back. I didn't know Etta Squire, but she had a gun in her hands, so she might shoot him, or at the very least kick him. Flotsam squirmed in my grip. Though he growled, he didn't attempt to snap at me.

As Watson's rumble joined in, Leo slipped his fingers inside Watson's collar as well.

"You've always been a pain, Leo." Etta glared at him and then at me. "Never interacted, but I've heard the same about you. Apparently the rumors are true." She let out a hacking cough, managed to keep the rifle steady on us, and didn't take her gaze away.

This wasn't good. I nearly laughed at the thought. Talk about an understatement. But it was true, nonetheless. Granted, there were two of us, but she had a gun. For one crazy moment, I considered hurling Flotsam at her, letting him use his fangs however he wanted, while I dove for her legs. Some crazy unexpected move that might catch her off guard enough to get the gun free.

And Katie's voice from the night before, warning Leo to take things slow whispered in my ear and held me in place.

Etta could have shot us already. So I had to believe that wasn't her plan. And if that was the case, then there might be a better moment to do something risky.

As if reading my thoughts, Etta took a couple of steps back. "I don't want to shoot you. Either of you. But one stupid move and I will." Though there was no tremble in her raspy voice, the rifle wavered in her declaration.

"You're not a killer, Etta." Leo spoke softly

beside me, and the barrel of the gun moved slightly in his direction.

"You don't know what I am." That time, her voice did tremble a bit.

Flotsam turned loose another round of barking and struggled in my arms once more, bringing the gun's focus back to us.

Leo started to stand.

"Don't even think about it!" Etta barked at him, swinging the rifle back to him and then returning it to Flotsam and me. "Put the muzzle back on that little demon."

I hesitated.

"Do it!" Etta shouted, which elicited a string of hacking and coughing. As she tried to get herself under control, she backed away several feet until she was in the center of the living room and far out of reach. "I'm sick of that mongrel. Don't tempt me. Put on the muzzle."

I did as she ordered, lowering my head to whisper apologies in Flotsam's big ears as he struggled to get free. Beside him, Watson licked his face through the metal cage. I was disheartened to see my fingers trembling as I fastened the clasps.

Leo's hand came to rest on my back, offering a bit of strength and reassurance.

Etta motioned toward the bathroom door with the rifle. "Put him back in there. Your fleabag too."

Maybe insanity took hold, but I started to argue, to demand that Watson stay with me, but then thought better of it. If he was out of sight, there would be less chance of her swinging the gun in his direction or kicking him, or a million other horrible possibilities that flitted through my mind.

I did as she said, having to push Flotsam through the bathroom door, and was grateful when Watson stayed without a power struggle, though he looked at me with judgment behind his fear-filled eyes. Shutting the two of them away in the bathroom nearly broke my heart.

"Now, get back on your knees, Fred."

I did as Etta commanded.

She glanced around the living room, the rifle trained on us. With Watson out of harm's way, I considered using her distraction and rushing down the narrow hallway and tackling her.

Again Leo's hand came to rest on my back.

Finally, taking another step back, Etta marked a path from where we were to the middle of the living room with the rifle. "Now both of you crawl in here. Hands and knees. When you get to the center, sit down."

We did as she demanded, exchanging glances as we crawled across the floor. Again, Leo must've been able to read my thoughts, my inclination to attack, as he gave a nearly imperceptible shake of his head.

"Good." Etta managed to keep the rifle aimed toward us with one hand, her shaky finger dangerously on the trigger, and pulled out her cell from her pocket with the other. "Now—"

Watson cut her off with a string of panicked and ferocious barks from the bathroom.

Etta flinched, and I thought for sure she was going to pull the trigger. "Shut that thing up or I will."

"Watson!" I practically screamed.

At the sound of my voice, Watson began to bark louder, more frantically.

No wonder, I sounded utterly terrified. Forcing some calm into my voice, I lowered the volume. "Watson! Be quiet."

He continued to bark.

"Come on, buddy." Leo called out soothingly. "Be quiet, Watson. No more barking."

He barked again, though the sound was hesitant.

"Watson!" I took the fear and the pleading from my voice as much as I could and infused a commanding tone I rarely used. "Be still!"

His barking trailed off into a pitiful whimper.

Etta nodded, tapped her phone, and lifted it to her ear. She was silent for a few moments as the call rang through. "Yeah. It's me. You'll never believe who showed at my place. The most irritating Smoky Bear you've ever seen and his truly annoying Nancy Drew."

She was silent for several more moments. Though I strained to hear, I couldn't make out what was said on the other end of the line.

Finally she nodded, slid the cell phone away, and brought her hand back up to steady the rifle once more.

I couldn't help but feel like we'd missed our chance.

She stared at us from the other side of the gun as she backed up a few more feet. "Sit on your hands too. No funny business."

Leo did as she asked.

I hesitated. Clearly whoever she'd called—I was willing to bet it was Chief Briggs—was on their way. Whenever he got here, the odds shifted from two against an older woman with a gun to two against an older woman with a gun, and a police chief with a gun who hated me with a passion. There might not be another moment to act.

"Fred." Leo didn't bother whispering, but his voice was soft and firm. "Don't."

The rifle trembled again in Etta's grip.

He risked sliding one of his hands out from underneath to touch mine. "Don't."

He was right. It might be the best odds we had, but they weren't odds at all. There was no way I could move from my seated position and make it across the living room before she shot one of us. If it had been just me, maybe I would've taken the chance. If it had been just me, I probably would've been shot already.

I sat on my hands.

As we waited, Etta didn't speak. Didn't rage, talk, or gloat. If anything, she looked sick to her stomach.

Leo must've noticed the same thing. "Etta, you don't have to do this. We've known each other for years. And I know you don't particularly like me, but—"

"Shut up, Leo." She coughed again.

"Etta." Leo's voice grew softer, calmer, more soothing. It didn't waver, and I didn't hear any fear. I had no idea how he did it. "It's not too late. Don't make things worse. You still have a choice. We can—"

Etta laughed. But it wasn't full of wicked glee,

not at all like some comic book villain. It was dark and sad and angry. And when she spoke, her voice trembled. "You have no idea. I've told you countless times that your rose-colored glasses needed to break before you got yourself in trouble. You should've listened."

"Etta."

"I said shut up, Leo!" The tremble was gone.

A million different plans, each one crazier than the previous flitted through my mind as we sat there. Sweat began to roll down my back. My phone rang in the pocket of my skirt. If Etta heard the vibrations, she didn't let on. I felt it go to voicemail. Then a few seconds later, it began to ring again.

Katie. It had to be Katie.

Somehow I'd forgotten. And thank God we'd made a contingency plan even though it had felt pointless to do so.

She tried one more time and then quit calling. She would help. No doubt.

Several more minutes passed; I had no idea how long. Every once in a while I heard twin whimpers from the bathroom, but Watson didn't bark again, and Flotsam couldn't.

With the length of time, somehow the panic began to fade, but it spiked again as we heard the engine of a vehicle, the crunch of tire over snow and gravel. Then the engine died. The sound of car doors slamming was followed by footsteps on the porch.

Chief Briggs sauntered through the front door of Etta's cabin, looking smug. Even though we'd guessed at it, his presence brought back a spike of fear. But it was the figure behind Briggs that made my heart leap into my throat.

Branson.

Katie had called him; he was here to save the day. Those were my first thoughts, but they lasted less than a heartbeat. His gaze flicked over Leo and me and then landed on Etta. "Good grief, you crazy old woman, can't you do anything right?"

"Give me the gun, Etta." Branson held out his hand as he walked toward her. "You're liable to blow us all to bits."

A spark of hope ignited in the darkness that washed over me when Branson walked in. He was taking the gun. We were going to be okay. He was undercover, playing a role. Maybe he had been the entire time. I just needed to give him a chance to turn the situation his way.

Etta practically shoved the rifle at Branson. "Take it! This is more than I ever wanted. I don't babysit dogs." She sneezed as if to prove her point and wiped her nose with the back of her arm. "I don't hold people at gunpoint. This isn't what I agreed to."

Beside me, Leo shifted.

"Quit complaining, Etta." Briggs rolled his eyes and dismissed her with bored disdain. He pulled his pistol from its holster and aimed it at us, his tone uninterested. "Don't try to be a hero, little park ranger."

I kept my gaze on the gun but felt Leo tense beside me and then settle back down.

With the rifle in his hands, Branson turned to face Chief Briggs. "What are you doing? There's no need for all of this. I guarantee you neither of them are armed."

I dared to glance at him, hoping to see some quick look my way, some secret message behind his eyes to tell me to be patient, that he had it under control. There was nothing, and his tone was just as bored as Briggs's.

The chief kept his pistol trained on Leo and me but gaped at Branson. "Are you kidding me with this? Do you think we're just going to sit here and lounge about in Etta's nasty little cabin and have tea?"

"I'm just saying there's no need to overreact. Neither of them is going to try anything stupid." Branson started to say something else, but Etta began sneezing again.

Briggs motioned from her to us. "Get yourself under control, Etta."

She glared at him through watery eyes but said nothing.

From the bathroom, Watson barked, and Flotsam joined in with high-pitched whimpering.

Chief Briggs cocked his head. "I thought you muzzled that thing." Etta didn't have a chance to respond before he looked at me. "Dear God, you brought your dog, didn't you?"

"Let Fred go." Still sitting on his hands, Leo shifted again, facing Briggs. "She doesn't have anything to do with this. She's not involved in the poaching. I'm the one who's—"

Briggs laughed. "You really are as original as cardboard, aren't you, Lopez? The whole *take me not her* thing?" He rolled his eyes. "Have you ever seen that work in any movie?"

I dared a glance in Leo's direction. Clearly he thought we were moments away from getting shot. Which... we were being held at gunpoint, but I couldn't accept that was how this was going to end. No way Branson would let it get that far. He'd blow his cover to save us. I had no doubt.

Leo remained focused on Briggs. "I don't know what deal you have with Etta, but I'll join in. What has she been doing for you? Helping the poachers get out of the park? Adjusting records, covering tracks? Whatever it is, count me in."

"Leo!" I hissed at him, partly in shock at what he was saying and also trying to get him to stop, to get him to give Branson a chance to figure this out.

He ignored me. "I guarantee you, I know the national park better than Etta. I'll make it worth your while. Just let Fred walk out of here, and I'll do whatever you tell me to do."

"Shut up, Leo." Branson sneered at him. "You're pathetic."

"*I'm* pathetic?" The placating tone vanished from Leo's voice. "*I'm* pathetic! You're the one wearing a badge, the one who put Fred in danger by lying to her this whole time!" Though I couldn't imagine how he managed, Leo sprang to his feet and charged at Branson. "If you even think—"

Chief Briggs swiveled the pistol in Leo's direction, and I lunged toward Leo to knock him out of the way.

Before Briggs could pull the trigger, Branson swung the rifle like a baseball bat, smashing Leo across the face with the handle.

The force of the impact caused Leo to spin backward. Unable to stop my forward motion, we collided, and he flipped over me, crashing to the floor with a groan.

Chief Briggs let out a loud guffaw of approval and clapped Branson on the back.

Spinning on my knees, I hurried to Leo. His nose was broken, and blood made its way down his face and onto the carpet. "Leo! Leo!" My hands roamed over his back and gripped his arm as he tried to push himself back up into a kneeling position. "Don't move. You're only going to hurt yourself more." I was vaguely aware of Watson barking like mad.

"Don't move, boy." Briggs's voice had gone cold. "The gun is trained on the back of your little girl-friend's head."

Leo froze and glared past me through an eye that was already beginning to swell shut. Then he met my gaze.

I just shook my head.

"Etta!" Branson's bark made me flinch. "Tie Leo up so he doesn't cause any more problems." There was a pause before Branson spoke again, his voice cold. "And gag him."

As Etta retrieved what she needed from a kitchen drawer and made her way over to Leo, I desperately tried to think through my options. There had to be something I could do to save us. There had to be. But not a single option came to mind. Trying to rush Briggs wouldn't work, clearly. The only thing I could see was to simply wait. Believe there would be some moment that I could take advantage of to get us out of this. Though I couldn't help but feel we'd already missed that moment when it had just been Etta and us. We should've gone for it then.

"You don't need to restrain Leo or gag him. He'll stay where he is." I kept one hand on Leo's back and turned to Briggs and Branson. Briggs did indeed have his pistol pointed right at my head, so I turned a beseeching gaze toward Branson. "Please."

There was no secret message in his green eyes, just coldness. "Sorry, Fred. It's not an option."

"It's okay, Fred." Leo's whisper was pained but firm behind me. "Let it happen." I heard the implied *save yourself.*

"You always were such an annoying little Boy Scout." Etta kneeled beside Leo and began to tie his arms behind his back. "I told you. Certain things in life aren't able to be changed, but you wouldn't listen."

I couldn't believe I wasn't fighting, that I stayed at Leo's side while he was bound and gagged and rendered powerless. But I was as well. I could think of no move that wouldn't make things worse.

"When you're done with that one, tie up Ms. Page here, and make sure you gag her properly. I've wanted her to shut up from the minute she came into town." As Briggs spoke to Etta, he grinned wickedly at me over the gun.

"No!" Branson stepped forward, almost like he was going to step in between the gun and me, but he didn't. He turned to look at Briggs. "There's no reason to do that. She's not going to attack, she is no danger." He shot a look my way. "You'll do what you're told, right?"

I finally saw what I'd been looking for, the man I thought I knew, in those green eyes. He was there, and he was pleading with me silently. Relief washed over me, but I tried not to let it show. I hadn't been wrong. "Right. I'll do what you tell me to."

There was a spark of relief in Branson's gaze, as if he'd expected me to argue or not understand, but then he faced Briggs once more. "See?"

Briggs gaped at Branson. "Seriously, Wexler? Still?" He gestured at me with the gun. "What is it about this woman? I don't get it? There's a whole lot prettier options in town, and this one's strung you along for months. Had you playing the part of a fool, and here you are, still acting like her little dog." Before Branson could respond, Briggs raised his voice to a near scream. "And speaking of, somebody shut up that dog! Or I will!"

In my panic and the blood pounding in my ears, I'd barely registered Watson's whaling.

"Watson!" I let out a wail of my own, and there was no keeping the tremble out of my voice. "Mom is okay. Be quiet, baby."

He barked again, just as loud, but the feel of it shifted slightly, turning almost questioning.

"Good boy, Watson. No more barking. Be quiet!" For the first time since Etta had appeared, I felt tears streaming down my cheeks, heard the pleading desperation in my voice. What had we been thinking, bringing Watson?

I knew what we'd thought, what we'd planned. None of this was supposed to happen.

"Watson! Be quiet!"

He barked again and then faded off into a constant whine.

I looked back at Briggs and lowered my voice. "Please don't hurt him. He hasn't done anything wrong. He won't—"

"What are you going to promise me, Ms. Page? It was pointless for Leo to try, but at least he had the potential of something. What do you think *you* have?" Again the look in Briggs's eyes left no doubt that he hated me, though I still didn't understand why. "Free books? Pastries from that annoying friend of yours?" He sneered at Branson before looking back at me. "Maybe you think you have some strange effect on men." He laughed. "Apparently you do, considering you have that idiot park ranger and a man I consider one of the smartest, cleverest men alive in any *other* way, groveling at your feet. Let me make it clear, you have the exact opposite effect on me."

Branson shot out a hand and grabbed Brigg's arm as the chief took a step in my direction. "Briggs. Knock it off."

The chief whirled back on him. For just a second, he lowered the gun, but before I could even consider whether I should leap, he leveled it at Leo. He didn't even have to look away from Branson, as if he'd read my mind and knew exactly how to stop me without a glitch in his concentration.

With his free hand, he jabbed at Branson's chest. "How do you expect this to go down, Wexler? That we're going to sit here and have a conversation and come to an understanding? Do you really think there's some happy ending for you in this with that obnoxious woman?"

"I'm saying calm down. Fred has done everything you've asked." Branson dropped his grip from the chief's arm and softened his tone. "She's not fighting back. She's not going to try anything crazy."

I was certain that was directed as a command to me almost as much as reassurance to Briggs.

"Let's just slow down. We can figure this out."

"Really?" A smirk played over the chief's face. "How exactly are we going to figure this out? You think no matter what they promise that we can just walk out of here and things will go back to normal?"

Etta sneezed again from behind me but didn't even cause a glitch in their debate.

"What I think, is that if we act too quickly, or make a rash decision, this whole thing is over. How are you going to explain a dead park ranger and a dead…" Branson's voice had been steady up until right then, and it broke. He shook his head. "Everything you've built in this town would be for nothing. You brought me here because I'm good at this. Like you said, I'm one of the smartest men you know, so trust me. We need to be smart about this."

Briggs was silent for several moments. He looked back and forth between Branson and me, keeping his pistol trained on Leo. "What I think, is that no matter how this plays out, things in Estes are done. What I *know* is that you need to turn your brain on.

Regardless of what comes next, these two know our part in this. And maybe you're not worried about that, but that's just because she has you under some sort of spell." He lifted his hand and tapped hard enough on Branson's temple to cause him to wince. "What delusion do you have in that head of yours? That somehow the two of you are going to skip away from this cabin to a happily ever after? She didn't even love you when she thought you were a knight in shining armor. You weren't good enough for her then. Why in the world do you think she'd accept you now?" He took a step from Branson and moved my way, shifting the barrel of the gun from Leo toward me.

Branson made a motion toward him but paused. Any move he made would end in my death.

Briggs knelt in front of me so we were eye to eye, and angled the gun toward my chest.

My tears over Watson had dried. I wasn't sure if he was barking again or not. Everything was static—the voices of Briggs and Branson loud and causing everything else to fade away. I tried to think. I could feel the clock ticking, feel it winding down. There wasn't going to be another moment.

I had to make a chance of my own. Somehow. Maybe... if Briggs got just a touch closer, I could somehow manage to use my legs to knock him off-balance while twisting my torso out of a bullet's trajectory.

Right, because I was a gymnast and lived in *The Matrix*.

Still, it was the only possible chance I saw. But he needed to get closer, just a little closer.

"Tell poor little Branson the truth, Winifred. You don't love him. You never did. You were just using him to help you play detective. Help you feel like you were Daddy's little girl." His smile was huge as he stared at me—like a shark. I could practically see him salivating over what was surely about to happen. "Tell him what you think of him now." Though he did nudge closer, he twisted the pistol slightly, centering it on my chest. "Even if there was a chance before, what about now, now that you know what he is?" He chuckled. "Maybe I'm giving you too much credit. Perhaps you have an effect on me after all and I'm making assumptions that you're smarter than you are." He shifted his weight, but still didn't move closer, his feet still out of reach of my legs. "Have you still not figured out that *Branson* killed Max? Not that you care about him. But what about all the others? What about our little traitor, Eddie? You liked that little rat, right?"

Despite my fear, I couldn't help but glance at Branson.

And I saw the truth in his eyes.

Briggs laughed again. "I see I was right. You are a moron. Couldn't even figure that out." He did scoot just a little closer then, just a touch. The gun was near enough that I could reach out and touch it. Maybe I could kick it?

"What do you think he was doing all those nights when he would just randomly disappear? A bunch of fishing trips? You're a detective's daughter—have you ever known a policeman to get that much vacation time?" His voice rose as he addressed Branson, but he didn't look away. "Ask her, Wexler. Ask her what she thinks of you now."

Branson didn't reply, though he came nearer.

I kept my gaze trained on Briggs's gun, waiting for it to get just a touch closer and I'd take my chance.

Briggs didn't look away from me. "Too much of a coward to ask, Wexler? That's okay. Once she's gone, you'll get back to normal. We can—"

The thunder of the rifle filled the little cabin.

One second Briggs was glaring into my eyes. The next, he was gone.

As if from a million miles away, Watson began

his frenzied barking once more, Leo made a muffled scream, and Etta started to yell.

The chief's dead body came into focus, sprawled at my feet. I looked up at Branson just in time to see him swing the rifle past me, and another shot filled the cabin.

I screamed and whirled around, attempting to throw myself in front of Leo, though I was already too late. I grabbed him, meeting his wide, shocked eyes, his muffled words barely reaching my ears, and then saw Etta sprawled on the floor behind him.

It was probably a matter of seconds, but it felt like endless minutes as I stared at her, waiting for my brain to override the fear and make sense of the picture. Even so I had to scan down Leo's body before trusting that there was no wound, that he wasn't shot.

I turned back to Branson as he lowered the rifle. It paused in its arc, at the point it was aimed at Leo. Before I could say anything, plead or shout, before I could throw myself in front of Leo, the rifle lowered farther and pointed at the floor. Branson's eyes met mine.

NINETEEN

"I thought..." I tore my gaze away from Branson's eyes, glanced at the rifle aimed at the floor and then back up. "I thought you were going to..." I shook my head. I couldn't finish the sentence, didn't need to. Spinning on my knees, I started to peel back the duct tape of Leo's gag, but the blood coming from his broken nose gave me pause, bringing back the image of Branson hitting Leo in the face with the butt of the rifle.

Leo's wide brown eyes, filled with panic and anger, tried to warn me as did his muffled words.

"Don't, Fred." I froze at Branson's hard words and looked over my shoulder, some crazed part of me expecting to see the rifle pointed at me again. It wasn't, but Branson hadn't dropped it to the floor either. "Leave him tied."

Everything had happened so fast, and yet it felt

like we'd been stuck in the cabin for weeks. A weird slow-motion whirlwind of drama, confusion, and panic. Even as I'd attempted to figure out how to survive—when to kick out at Chief Briggs, to determine if we'd missed our chance—the back of my mind had been shoving puzzle pieces together. Though I hated the picture it formed, it was the only one that made sense. "You weren't undercover with them? You weren't playing a role?"

He didn't budge. "You're smarter than that."

Yes, I was. Though apparently not smart enough, considering how long it'd taken me to figure it out. Not that I'd *figured* anything out. It'd been shoved in my face. Without looking at Briggs or Etta, I motioned behind me. "But if you're part of them... you just killed..."

He shrugged as if he had done nothing more than smash a spider. Despite that, for the first time since I'd met him, worry and fear appeared in those bright green eyes. His voice didn't betray those emotions. "Briggs was going to kill you."

So it was that simple. "Etta wasn't. She didn't even have a gun."

"No, she wasn't." He didn't give any other explanation.

"You're not going to...?"

Hurt flashed in his eyes, superimposing itself over the worry and fear. "I've always told you that you are safe with me."

Yes. He had.

I turned back to Leo, reaching for the duct tape covering his mouth.

"I said leave him tied!"

Watson began barking like crazy from the bathroom.

Promises of being safe or not, I flinched at Branson's shout of command. As I faced him once more, I repositioned myself so I was directly between him and Leo. "You're not going to hurt him."

Though it wasn't a question, Branson treated it as one. "No, I'm not." He sounded disappointed. "You and I need to talk. I'm not having his interference when we do."

Maybe my nerves were on the edge of breaking, doubtlessly. Perhaps it was the combination of fear, relief, exhaustion, and adrenaline, I had no clue, but whatever it was, he sparked my anger and I laughed.

That time, *he* flinched.

"Are you kidding me? You sound just like you did when you would order me off a case. Has it ever worked for you? Have I *ever* listened when you bark orders at me?" I gestured at the rifle. "I'm untying

Leo, and he needs medical attention. Did you forget hitting him in the face with that thing?"

"I most definitely haven't forgotten." Branson smirked as he took a step forward. "And me hitting him in the face was the only thing that saved his life. The only reason I did that was because I knew you wouldn't forgive me if he died."

That took my words away for a second until the muffled sounds of whatever Leo was trying to say brought me back to him. Once more, I turned and started to gently remove the tape.

Branson cursed. "He's fine, Fred! Give us a few minutes to talk. You and me. Without his stupid interference."

I didn't look back, just used the fingertips of my left hand to gently smooth out the bruising skin of Leo's cheek while trying to take off the tape as pain-lessly as I could with my right.

"Please, Fred."

There was a pleading in Branson's voice that almost made me pause, but I didn't.

"Just a few minutes before I have to—"

The crunch of tires pulling to an abrupt halt, accompanied by the sound of gravel and ice spraying against the small cabin, froze all three of us in place.

There was the slamming of doors and pounding footsteps.

I twisted toward the doorway.

Watson's barks were beginning to sound hoarse.

Branson lifted and aimed the rifle at the door and steadied his stance.

The door was flung open and Katie rushed in. "Fred!" She came to a screeching halt when she saw the barrel of the gun, but then she was shoved forward several stumbling steps as Paulie smashed into her. He too froze.

Every emotion I'd been feeling was echoed in Katie's eyes as she lifted her gaze from the barrel of the gun to Branson, then looked over to me, to Leo, and to the bodies on the floor, before finally back to Branson. I couldn't help but have a shot of pride for my best friend when she tilted her chin and anger filled her voice. "I called you to help. I called *you* to help her!" She took a step forward in her anger and paused. When she spoke again, her voice trembled slightly as it lowered in volume. "When Fred still wasn't answering her phone and you weren't answering yours, I went to Paulie. He told me... He told me that you..." Tangible disgust filled every part of her. "Even so, he said Fred would be safe with you. But here you are with—"

"I did help her. She's alive, isn't she?" I almost thought I heard guilt in Branson's voice.

"So now what?" Katie cocked an eyebrow at him. "You kill the rest of us and take her?"

Behind her, Paulie put a hand on Katie's shoulder as if telling her not to give Branson any ideas.

For several moments, Branson actually seemed to consider, but then he used the rifle to motion Katie and Paulie toward Leo and me. "Get over there with them. Kneel down."

Katie took another step forward. "You've got to be kidding me if you think I'm going to—"

"Do it!" Branson screamed in a tone I'd never dreamed would come from him—full of anger, fury.

They did, both of them. Paulie kneeled beside me, with Katie on the other side of Leo, her hand coming to rest on his back.

Branson nodded his approval before his eyes met mine once more and his expression softened for just a second. I could see he was saying something, trying to get me to understand, but I couldn't. His eyes hardened again. "Toss your cell phones to me. All of you. And keys."

Paulie complied instantly, pulling it out of his pocket and sliding it to Branson.

After a moment, Katie did the same with hers, her key ring as well.

I debated for a few seconds, maybe it was foolish, but I did believe I was safe with him. So much so that I thought I could pull out the cell phone, call the police, and he wouldn't hurt me. But he *was* the police. I wasn't so certain he wouldn't hurt one of the others to make me obey. I wouldn't have thought such a thing possible before, but... things had changed...

I slid the cell from the pocket of my skirt and noticed countless missed calls from Katie. I hadn't even felt them coming through after her first couple of tries. I tossed it toward Branson.

He motioned toward Leo. "His too."

Without waiting, Katie reached into the pocket of his jeans as Leo twisted and raised his hips to give her better access, and then his phone and keys joined the others at Branson's feet.

Branson kept the gun trained on us as he kneeled on one knee to retrieve the cell phones, each one disappearing into various pockets. When he stood again, his eyes met mine once more. "Don't follow me."

He lowered the gun, turned, and walked toward

the door, completely unconcerned that any of us would try to tackle him.

We didn't. All of us remained frozen exactly where we were as Watson's barks continued to fill the cabin.

Then Branson was gone, leaving the door open behind him and letting the bright cold day rush in. None of us moved a muscle until we heard the rumble of a car and its retreat as it drove away.

As one, Katie and I clicked into motion. Me working on the duct tape as Katie began untying Leo's wrists and legs.

Just as I pulled out the sock that had been stuffed into Leo's mouth, Watson crashed into me, nearly knocking me over. I caught myself in time to avoid landing on Leo and wrapped my arms around Watson, burying my face in his fur as he barked and licked and whimpered. "Oh, sweetie, I—" My throat constricted, cutting off my words as tears finally began to fall.

Paulie emerged from the hallway. Fat, fluffy Flotsam cradled in his arms like a baby, muzzle-free and lathering Paulie's face with kisses as he washed away the tears that streamed down his cheeks.

"It's okay, Fred. We're all okay." Leo was sitting up, and he wrapped an arm around my shoulders, pulling me to him. He did the same with Katie on the other side. "It's over."

Watson darted a quick lick over Leo's face, which made Leo wince, and then Watson returned to me.

I angled so I could see Leo's face. "You're hurt."

He shrugged. "I've broken my nose before. Though I'm betting I have a nice old concussion, judging from the headache. Who knows, maybe a skull fracture." Another shrug like it wasn't a big deal, and then he grinned. "Better than the alternative."

Katie lifted her hand to his cheek but stopped before making contact. "Your teeth, they're chipped."

Sure enough, three of his top teeth had chipped, ruining his perfect smile. Again he shrugged. "We don't get paid a lot being park rangers, but we've got killer dental insurance." The humor left his eyes as he held mine. "Are you okay?"

"You were here. You know I'm okay. You took all the—"

"That's not what I meant." His brown gaze darted to the door and then back.

I simply nodded.

I wasn't sure if I was.

Paulie sat in front of us, Flotsam still in his lap,

tears continuing to stream, though they seemed to have changed from those of relief to guilt. "I'm so sorry. I'm *so* sorry." He sounded close to hyperventilating. "I've hated lying to you, to all of you. But..."

Katie leaned forward and rubbed his knee. "They had Flotsam. We understand."

He nodded frantically and dipped his head to wipe his eyes as best he could on his arm, clearly unwilling to take either hand from Flotsam. "It's not just that." He sniffed and looked at me. "I've never been able to tell you everything. I've always known... but I couldn't..." He spoke between sobs and then seemed to give up.

More puzzle pieces fell into place, filling the gaps in Paulie's story once we'd finally figured out why he'd come to Estes, why he'd used a fake name. The ferocity Branson had displayed when I'd attempted to look into Paulie's past. Paulie telling me there were still secrets in town, things he couldn't say, but that he'd tell me if I was in danger.

Watson had finally begun to calm, but I kept stroking him as I addressed Paulie. "Were you under Briggs and Branson's control before you got to Estes or after?"

"After." He choked out another sob. "I came here

under police protection, to be safe, to start again, and then got here... only to find I wasn't safe at all."

Leo's hand joined Katie's on Paulie's knee. "You are now. You're safe now."

Paulie attempted a smile, almost succeeded.

The four of us sat there, dazed, cuddling and reassuring the two dogs, taking comfort from them, as we tried to come to grips with what had just happened.

Once more, time played the game where a couple of minutes felt like hours. But however much of it passed, the reality of our surroundings crowded in again—the little cabin, Etta, Chief Briggs.

"How do we get out of here? It's a long, long walk back into town." Katie kept her eyes averted from the bodies.

"I have the CB in the Jeep. I'll call for help." Leo stood, groaned in pain, and held his head.

"I can do it, Leo." Katie started to stand. "You shouldn't be moving."

He waved her off with a pained smile. "I'm fine."

I inspected Leo. He did seem fine. He would need to get checked out, but he seemed like himself. "The question is, who do we get help from? We can't call the police." I looked at Paulie. "Can we? Is it just Briggs and Branson? Or are there others?"

He shrugged. "Briggs and Branson were the only ones I had contact with. They were the ones who would tell me what they wanted me to do." He glanced at Etta. "I knew about her, but..." Paulie refocused on me. "I know there are more people involved in town, but I don't know who they are. I don't think anyone's as high up as Branson and Briggs, but I can't say."

"Seriously?" Leo had made it to the doorway and turned back. He had to grip the doorjamb at his swift movement. "Then who do we call? Maybe nobody. Maybe we walk back to town. Who knows who'd be listening if I use the CB. If none of the police can be trusted, then we could just end up with another rifle in our faces."

"Brent Jackson wouldn't be involved in this. I'd swear to it." I glanced at Katie for confirmation, and she nodded. "He nearly died protecting Katie and me."

"As far as I know, Briggs and Branson are the only police that were involved. They made certain to tell me never to talk to any of the other officers about anything. Not to call them for help, nothing." Paulie nodded at Leo. "I think we'll be okay with the police."

Another thought hit me. "So... Susan?"

Paulie almost smiled. "She definitely wasn't in on it. Briggs hated her."

"That makes sense. She was the only one who'd take me seriously when I called about the poaching."

As Leo continued toward the Jeep, I placed Watson on the floor, and we headed out after him.

Katie, Paulie, and Flotsam followed.

Within a few minutes, we were all huddled on the porch, under large packing blankets Leo kept in his Jeep. The cold was preferable to waiting inside the cabin.

Another few minutes passed before three police cars made their way up the gravel road. Susan Green and Brent Jackson exited the first one and walked toward us. Officer Jackson's face was filled with concern and he went directly to our little group.

Susan marched right past us, eyes straight ahead, and walked into the cabin. At least that was her intention. She gasped, a sound I'd never heard Susan Green make and froze in the doorway. After surveying what lay inside, she looked back, and to my surprise, her eyes met mine. "Branson was one of them?"

I nodded.

After a second, she did as well. "Explains a lot."

The Cozy Corgi had never felt so good. There'd been the typical morning rush from the locals as they got their coffee, pastries, and gossip. As per normal, anytime that gossip was particularly juicy, the rush lasted nearly till noon.

From my spot at the counter of the bookshop, I watched Watson napping in his favorite spot, the radiant November light filtering through the window, warming him. Beyond him, huge, fluffy snowflakes drifted slowly across Elkhorn Avenue. Somewhere behind me, Ben laughed gently as he helped a young woman pick out a meditative coloring book. The soft chatter of voices and clatter of pans from Katie's bakery overhead drifted down along with the comforting aroma of yeast and sugar. The fireplaces crackled and popped, just barely audible over the piped-in music of the Mills Brothers "I'll Be Around."

After everything was said and done the night before, the four of us didn't want to part. After being cleared by the doctor, Leo and Katie helped me make dinner at my house, and Paulie brought the dogs. Before we knew it, Athena dropped by, as did my parents and my uncles. Long after everyone else left, Katie, Leo, and I curled up on the couch, Watson snoring by the fire, and we slept through endless reruns of Katie's favorite, *The Great British Bake Off*.

Though it had been wonderful to be surrounded by people I loved in my own home and feeling safe, being in the Cozy Corgi was better. Working, returning to normal. Some part of me wanted to grieve over Branson's betrayal, wanted to scream in rage. Another part felt like the biggest fool in the world. And some other little portion whispered that somehow, somewhere, some part of me had known, had warned. I shoved all of that aside—it was too much to deal with at that moment. I knew it would come up at some point, but there was no reason to face it then.

Watson's paws twitched in his sleep, and I wondered what he was dreaming. I didn't think he was reliving any of the moments from the day before, the gentle smile on his muzzle seemed pleasant enough. Chances were he was having visions of a parfait of various offerings from Katie's baking, with a couple of his favorite all-natural dog bone treats in between every layer. I hoped.

I decided he had the right idea. Katie and Nick were happily baking away overhead, and Ben was helping the only customer in the bookshop, so it was the perfect time for me to curl up on the antique sofa in front of the fire in *my* favorite location. It didn't even matter which mystery I pulled off the shelves. I just needed the weight of a book in my hands and to get carried away on someone else's adventure.

I started to turn and head to the mystery room, when the front door opened and Delilah walked through, flanked by four women. All five were wearing their silk Pink Panther jackets. The woman to Delilah's left was Nadiya Hameed, and she held hands with the larger blonde beside her.

"Well, Winifred Page, looks like luck is on our side." Delilah practically slithered across the hardwood floor. "I was afraid you'd already found a new dead body and wouldn't be here."

Some of the ease I'd been feeling evaporated at the sight of Delilah's little club. It didn't matter that

I'd be forty in less than a year, or that I was a strong, independent woman, as Anna had put it. I couldn't help but feel that nagging insecurity left over from middle school as I walked by the cool girls' table and prayed they wouldn't see me. Although, as I glanced at the larger blonde and then at a couple of the others, I had to admit the difference. Despite Delilah's and Nadiya's pinup beauty status, the group wasn't entirely made up of Barbie dolls. Not even close.

I reminded myself that I'd looked down the barrel of a gun the day before, and this was nothing compared to that. And I was most definitely *not* still in middle school. "No, no dead bodies today. Just lots of dirty chais and pastries."

"As it should be. You deserve it." Delilah's smile turned from teasing to casually friendly. As she reached the counter, I looked over the group's shoulders and saw Watson lift his head, inspect, and then sink back down with a tired sigh. "We all took the day off work to celebrate Nadiya's release, and we wanted to come down and say thank you."

Nadiya let go of the blonde's hand and adjusted her glasses as she walked around the counter. She hesitated, and I thought she was about to stick out her hand, but instead she practically flung herself my way and wrapped her arms around me, trapping my arms at my side. "I can't thank you enough." She trembled.

Feeling awkward, I glanced around for some sort of rescue as I attempted to pat Nadiya but only succeeded in patting my own thigh. Delilah caught my gaze, and I could tell she was about to chuckle. Finally Nadiya pulled away and looked up at me. "You don't have anything to thank me for, Nadiya. I didn't figure it out. Everything I uncovered made you look guilty, honestly. If it weren't for Leo, I would've given up and said that the police were right. That you are the one who killed Max."

"I wanted to." She laughed and took a step back but didn't return to the other side of the counter. "And I'm thankful for Leo. But I'm also thankful for you. You may not have figured it out, but you didn't give up, and because of that"—she shrugged—"things went down in a way that cleared my name."

"I'm glad it worked out as it should've." Again thoughts of Branson threatened in the back of my mind, and I shoved them away. It hurt. I didn't want to hurt, or be angry. "And I'm sorry that you were in jail for something you didn't do."

"I intended to." She pushed up her glasses again, and she shrugged once more and laughed. "Well, I wasn't actually going to *kill* either of the poachers, but I was going to hold them at gunpoint until the police arrived."

"So you were going after them that night?"

Nadiya nodded. "Yeah. I heard the call on the scanner, saying that your bookshop had been broken into by the poachers. That they suspected they were heading to the dispensary in Lyons. That's where I went. That's where Sergeant Wexler found me and arrested me."

She'd given them the perfect scapegoat. "Was it your gun beside you as they said?"

"No. Mine was in the glove compartment. I didn't even have a chance to get it out." A hardness came into her dark brown eyes, and some of the anger that was apparent on her social media accounts flitted into her voice. "It's ridiculous. I think Max Weasel got *exactly* what he deserved. But I didn't do it." A dark grin split her beautiful lips. "Who knows, maybe it's for the best. My time in solitary confinement for the past few days might make it where if I ever run into Max's nasty brother, I won't give him what he deserves. Maybe."

Solitary confinement. And again, it all made sense. No wonder Branson wouldn't let anyone talk to her.

"There's a lot more creative ways to get revenge on men than killing them, Nadiya. Stick with me—I'll teach you." Delilah pulled the focus back to her once more, and again when she smiled at me, there was genuine affection and not even a hint of humor. "You'd make a great Pink Panther, Fred. Maybe the color of the jacket wouldn't exactly go with your hair, but..." She tilted her head and squinted her blue eyes, "I think you could pull it off."

That junior high girl still inside me, whispering insecurities, did a happy dance and pumped her fists in the air. "Thank you, but the answer is still no. I'm more of a book club kinda gal."

A couple of hours later, Watson sprang up from his nearly unending nap when Mom and Barry came into the shop. With a happy bark, he scurried over, going so fast that he slid over the hardwood floor and crashed into Barry's legs. He did that so often, I was starting to think it was intentional.

Barry ripped off his jacket as if it was too much clothing, revealing his silver-and-teal tie-dyed tank top, and bent to greet Watson with adequate enthusiasm. "I wish everybody in the world was as happy to see me as you are, little man."

Mom patted Barry's head lovingly from where he knelt and came to meet me as I walked in from where I'd been reading in the mystery room. She wrapped me up in another hug. I had a feeling I was going to be getting even more of those than normal from her for a while. "Fred." She whispered my name and just hung on.

Her hug didn't feel awkward. If anything, it threatened to make me think about all the things I didn't want to think of. Made me want to pull my tiny mother onto the couch in front of the fire and just talk and talk and talk until she magically fixed everything like I'd thought she was able to do when I was small. Instead I just stroked her long silver hair, my heart swelling at the remaining streak of auburn in the strands.

From the corner of my eye, I noticed Ben sneak up the steps to the bakery, probably giving us privacy.

After a moment, Barry followed, squeezing my shoulder as he passed, Watson right on his heels.

Then it was just me and Mom, and still she held on.

"Are you okay?" I didn't attempt to pull back to look at her, just kept stroking her hair. "You know

I'm fine. We were together last night. I'm not in any danger."

She only nodded against my shoulder.

After a little while, she cleared her throat, and with a final squeeze stepped back. Tears brimmed in her eyes, but they didn't fall. "I don't think it really hit me at your house. Not really. Somewhere in the dead of night, I woke up in a complete panic. All of it crashing down right then."

"Mom." I took her hand. "You should've called me. You could've come over."

She shook her head. "No. You needed your sleep, your rest. And I had Barry." She touched my blouse, right over where the necklace she'd made hung beneath. "Plus I knew you were okay. The danger had passed."

I'd had my own panicked thought in the middle of the night. I'd woken cold on the couch, Katie and Leo both asleep at opposite ends, the never-ending baking show still playing on the television. It had taken a while to fall back to sleep. I told myself I wasn't going to bring it up to Mom for a good long while, but now that she was in front of me again, I couldn't help it. "It's another connection to the Irons family, Mom. *Here* in Estes. And Branson was part of it. I can't even take it all in. The fact that he's connected to Dad's murder, I—"

"It doesn't mean he's connected to your dad's murder. The organization is, but Branson and Briggs probably had nothing to do with Charles. The Irons crime family is huge, all over the nation. Your dad was just investigating that one small part of it." Her hands shot up suddenly to clasp both of my cheeks. "Don't go chasing the Irons family, Fred. Don't you dare."

The thought hadn't even entered my mind. Though it did then.

And Mom could see it. She gave a slight shake. "Don't you dare! You listen to me. I lost your father. I nearly lost you last night, *not* for the first time. It's hard enough knowing that you're looking into all these murders, that you've got enough of your father in you that you can't let it go. But I'm begging you. Focus on your life here. Don't go chasing danger."

"But they *are* here, Mom." Why couldn't I just be a good daughter and simply say yes to soothe her? "They are in Estes."

"*Were.*" Still she wouldn't let my face go. "They *were* in Estes. Briggs is dead, and Branson is gone. Please let that be enough."

I hadn't told her what Paulie said about there still

being connections in Estes Park, though he didn't know who they were. And I wasn't going to. Maybe I wasn't such a bad daughter after all. "Okay, Mom. Okay."

She studied my gaze as if looking for some deceit, then finally nodded and released my face. "Okay."

At that moment, the door opened again, and both of us looked around. Leo walked in, snow over the shoulders of his park ranger uniform. He smiled when he saw us, his chipped teeth looking out of place on his handsome face. "Guess who got promoted?"

"You did!" Mom's voice shot up happily as she clapped. I couldn't help but marvel at her a little bit. How quickly she'd stuffed it all away again. I never forgot how tough she was, not really. She might present as flighty and ever increasingly whimsical, but she had a core of steel every bit as strong as my father. "Well deserved, I'd say."

"*I'd say* it's more of a matter of protocol than anything else. They gave me Etta's position." He winked at my mom. "But thank you for the congratulations." He accepted a hug from her and then bugged his eyes out at me. "They *also* offered me her cabin, said I could live there rent-free. Apparently it's owned by the national park, which I didn't know."

I couldn't even pretend to hold back my shudder at the thought, but managed to come up with a positive response. "No rent. That's..." Okay, half a positive thought.

"Are you kidding? You couldn't pay me to live there. Not after yesterday." He glanced toward the stairs. "Katie here? I thought she'd get a kick out of it."

"Of course she is, baking away." I started to step aside so he could head up. "Actually, I could do with another dirty chai. Mom and I will join you. Maybe get some pastries while we're at it."

Mom grabbed my arm and gasped. "Leo, look!" She pointed to the front windows.

Leo and I both followed her gesture and gave little gasps of our own.

As one, the three of us crossed the store and stopped at the window. Outside, walking down the middle of the street in the dying light of day, between the streetlamps as they sputtered, as the snow drifted down, a ram walked ahead of his harem of ewes.

"Well, look at that," Leo whispered quietly, but even so, his wonder was clear.

It wasn't unusual to see elk and sheep walk through the downtown of Estes Park, even a bear or mountain lion wasn't overly newsworthy, but as the ram paused right in front of the Cozy Corgi, the snow gathering on his curling horns, and looked our way, there was no denying the moment was magic.

Masses of swirling stars filled the crystalline night sky over the white peaked mountains as the full moon illuminating the forest glistened off the freshly fallen snow covering the pines. Even the winding trail of footprints Watson and I left in our wake sparkled. The only sounds were the crunch of our feet cutting through the deep powder and Watson's easy breathing.

Over the past week, I'd taken to bookending our days. The morning walk through the woods that surrounded my cabin had become routine over the last few months, but once in town, even after hours spent surrounded by books, pastries, and friends, I discovered my soul needed some solitude to be able to settle down. The quiet companionship of my little grump in the winter forest helped.

Maybe it was strange that I wasn't experiencing

flashbacks of the rifle pointed at my face, of being certain the end was near, but I wasn't. Perhaps that was because even in those moments where I saw no possible escape, some part of me simply hadn't accepted the inevitable. Though, it hadn't been inevitable.

No, it wasn't fear that kept trickling in. True to form, it was my anger that continued to boil. I'd read someplace that anger wasn't really a primary emotion, that it covered up what was real below it— either betrayal, loneliness, embarrassment, whatever.

It didn't really matter. I felt how I felt. And I couldn't help but admit I'd played the part of the fool. How had I not realized? It all seemed so obvious in retrospect.

Branson's random nights and days away that seemed to happen spur of the moment? He was out doing the bidding of the Irons family. Duh! Okay, maybe that wasn't exactly obvious. I would've had to be truly paranoid to have leapt to that conclusion, but still. His waffling support? One minute gung-ho on me looking into a murder and the next causing whiplash as he set his foot down and demanded I keep my nose in my own business. From that perspective, it was easy to see which ones he'd been involved in and which ones he hadn't. And that, I thought, was what made me feel like the biggest fool of all. Clearly he'd been involved in some of the murders I'd looked into, at least in some fashion, and I hadn't noticed.

And to think I just sloughed off Chief Briggs. He hadn't been off the mark. As a detective's daughter, I knew how the police force felt about civilians shoving their way into an investigation. His hatred of me seemed a little extreme, but I hadn't given it much more thought than that. Besides, Susan Green hated my guts, and Paulie still swore that she'd never been part of it. From her reaction at the cabin, I believed him.

And of course, that was all cerebral.

The other part, the one that was harder to consider and even harder to admit, was that I'd considered giving Branson Wexler my heart. I'd nearly fallen for him. Nearly chose to ignore the warning signs and the little whisper of that voice. Nearly let all those who told me I was being unreasonable and throwing away a good thing convince me.

I hadn't, ultimately. So that was something. But I wished I hadn't even come close.

Maybe I was being too hard on myself.

I stopped at the edge of the forest where the

clearing opened to my little cabin. Watson plodded ahead a couple of yards before coming to the end of his leash and glaring back at me in irritation. I grinned at him but leaned against the tree. I took a few more seconds to give thanks for the life I'd built in Estes, the life I was building. It was going to look different than it had so far, but... that proved that it was a life.

Even though it was only the second week of November, Mom and Barry, assisted by Verona and Zelda, had come over a couple of nights before and helped me put up my Christmas tree. They said I needed some brightness. They'd been right.

From my spot against the tree outside, I had to admit that my grandparents' old cabin now looked like a Thomas Kincaid painting, surrounded by stars and snow-laden mountains and trees. Thick blankets of the stuff covered the roof and porch. I'd left the lights on, so the windows glowed warm and inviting, and the Christmas tree sparkled from within frosted windowpanes.

Not all aspects of my life were picture-perfect, but more than enough of them were. Within five minutes, I'd be in my nightclothes, curled up in front of the fire with a book and Watson snoring at my feet. And that would be enough.

Watson gave a little tug, and I answered with a roll of the eyes and then conceded. "Fine, Your Highness. Ruin a perfectly magical moment."

As we drew nearer to the porch, Watson began to pull harder at the leash and growled.

"Good grief, Watson. You're getting more demanding every day." I sped up. He had a point. Now that I was picturing a fire, I had to admit how cold it was outside.

I flung open the door to the cabin, pounded my snow boots on the mat, and was met with a pleasant wave of warmth.

Watson's growl increased, and I finally recognized the warning sound that had been there all the time.

Branson sat in the overstuffed armchair, his handsome features highlighted from his spot by the fireplace. Considering the seismic shift in my view of him, it threw me off how normal he looked in his dark-wash jeans and soft brown sweater.

He smiled. "I hope you don't mind. I helped myself. I thought the night called for a fire." He gestured at the little side table. "And hot chocolate. It won't be as good as what you make, but I did my best."

My heart raced, startled at finding him sitting,

unannounced, in my home. Wounded by the familiarity. And then an image of the rifle barrel flashed in my mind. I took a step back before I realized what I was doing.

"You're safe, Fred." Branson didn't move, and he glanced down at a growling Watson. "I don't blame you for being angry, little one, but I've always told you, your mama is safe with me. She still is." Those bright green eyes flicked back to me. "Always will be."

"What are you doing here?" I remained in the doorway.

"I wanted to talk. I wanted to see you."

As if nothing had happened. I glanced behind me, looking for tracks that should have alerted me; there were none. Just departing and returning sets of Watson's and my own. He must've come in through the back. "You broke into my house."

Branson nodded. "Yes, that's true." He smiled, *he actually smiled*. It held a hint of humor and affection. "Don't worry, I didn't steal anything. I'm not a thief."

"No. Just a murderer." The words were out before I considered, but I had no desire to take them back.

His smile faltered, but the expression in his eyes remained calm, kind. "Yes. That's also true." He casually picked up one of the mugs of hot chocolate and took a sip. "Sadly, not as good as yours. Can we talk?"

I should have run, snatched up Watson, rushed to the Mini Cooper, and driven away as fast as possible while calling the police at the same time.

Instead I walked into the house, closed the door, unleashed Watson—who stayed by my side, growling —and removed my jacket, scarf, and snow boots. If I called the police, he'd be gone into the wind. They wouldn't have a chance. And I knew, without a shadow of a doubt, that I truly was safe with Branson. Plus, I wanted to talk to him too.

My heart still pounding like a twelve-piece band, I crossed the living room, accepted the hot chocolate, and then sat on the couch across from him. In a very un-Watson-like move, Watson leaped onto the couch and snuggled beside me, resting his head on my lap and keeping a wary gaze on Branson.

We sat in silence for several minutes, or maybe seconds, I had no idea. We sipped our hot chocolate. He was right, it wasn't as good as mine, but decent. After the first taste another warning went off, at how stupid I had to be drinking something he offered me. But again, I was safe with him. I just was, so I sipped again.

He shifted nervously. "You know, I'm not really sure where to begin now that we're here."

"You're associated with the Irons crime family, right?" Though I felt a bigger fool because of the romantic notions I'd had for him, those paled in comparison to my chief concern.

He grinned. "Okay, I guess we'll start there. And yes, I am."

"So does that mean you were..." I caught myself. I did know I was safe with him, but the man had lied to me from the moment I'd met him, so I narrowed my eyes and leaned forward slightly. "If I ask you questions, will you be honest with all of them?"

He didn't even hesitate. "Yes. You deserve that. If you ask something I'm not willing to or can't answer, then I'll say that. But I can promise you, I will never lie to you again."

Again... I nearly snorted in disgust but held it back. I started to repeat the question and then realized my emotions were about to get the best of me, so I took a couple more seconds, some slow breaths, and another sip or two of hot chocolate, then began again, my voice steady. "Were you involved with my father's murder?"

"No." Though Branson winced, he didn't hesitate then either. "I was already working for the Irons family at that time, but I've never been stationed in Missouri. I wasn't part of it. Honestly, I didn't even know about it. Sure, about the bust and how it affected... business, but I wasn't aware of the details or the players. Not until later."

I studied him, hard and long, and I believed him. A larger wave of relief than I would've expected washed over me. It only lasted for a second. "Did you know from the beginning, when you met me at the first murder in the Cozy Corgi? You knew who I was? Who my father was?"

"No." Branson held my gaze and leaned forward like he was going to stretch across the distance to take my hand. He didn't go that far, thankfully. "I didn't know, Fred. Not then."

Some of the relief came back, though I couldn't exactly say why it mattered. It wouldn't change what was. "When did you know?"

He shrugged. "I can't say. I don't remember the exact moment. But not too long after that."

"Before you asked me to dinner?" *Good grief!* Why was this so important?

"No, I didn't know then." Branson winced once more, then sighed. "I did know by the time we actually went to dinner at Pasta Thyme. But by then, I'd already fallen for you."

That stung, and then I realized why it did matter. "You went out with me, knowing that you were involved with my father's murder."

"Not directly, I wasn't." He was matter-of-fact.

I stared at him. I couldn't believe his reaction. He was part of the Irons crime family.

"*Charles Franklin* was involved in your dad's..." He cocked his head. "I just realized that he and your father both had the same first name. Strange." His tone returned to normal. "Anyway, Charles Franklin was involved in your dad's murder, though I don't know if he's the one who actually killed him."

I thought I knew where he was going, but I couldn't bring myself to prompt or urge him to stop.

"You know that we killed Franklin during a police shootout in Glen Haven after he went rogue and tried to hurt Paulie." His eyes held mine, maybe daring me to look away, or begging me to see the truth. "When I shot him, it was partly for you, for your father."

I stared at him, speechless for several moments. My emotions were so all over the place I couldn't come close to landing on one of them. "Am I supposed to thank you for that?"

My whisper must've sounded strange, as Watson looked up at me in concern.

Another gentle smile played on Branson's face, but he didn't respond.

More for something to do than anything, I took another sip of hot chocolate, and though I wasn't a big drinker, I wished he'd spiked it with something stronger. I couldn't take thinking about my father anymore. Branson had already said he didn't know who killed my dad. What did any of the rest matter? "Is what Briggs said true? You killed Eddie?"

He laughed softly, but it wasn't a mocking sound. "You had a strange soft spot for that weird little drug dealer."

Yes, I supposed I did, though that wasn't how I'd thought of him. He'd simply been a charming hipster who'd owned a dispensary, hero-worshiped my step-father, and had been kind to Watson and me.

Branson didn't wait for more prompting. "Yeah, I did." He shrugged once more, and I had to marvel that as he spoke of murder, his tone was so casual. There was no hint of guilt or aggression. It was all matter-of-fact. "There was no other choice when it came to light he'd been going behind our back, selling produce to Sid at a cut-throat rate. He was the same as Owen, poaching those birds for his own profit behind our back." He shrugged. "As you know, someone else helped me out with that one, though unintentionally."

I'd guessed at the reason. It had been one of the things that had plagued me all week, the memory of telling Branson what I'd discovered about Eddie. When I'd told him, I'd thought Branson's anger had been about drugs filtering into his town, not that he wasn't the only source. I knew I wasn't responsible for Eddie's death, but... I'd helped ignite the fuse. I pushed on.

"So the person in jail..." My intellect caught up with my words. I'd never seen proof of an arrest for Eddie's murder. Branson had said it was solved and justice had been served. I'd simply believed him and moved on. "There's no one in jail for Eddie's murder, is there?"

He shook his head with a sad smile. "No."

Just another lie. I moved on. "And Max? Is his brother dead too?"

He sighed. "Fred"—he motioned toward the doorway—"you said it yourself, right there. I'm a murderer. Do you really want the list? It's a long one. I'll give it to you if you want. How much time do you have?"

I warred with attempting to shove everything I knew about the man to one picture. I believed the gentleness and kindness I'd seen in him, *felt* from him, was genuine, but so was this—that he could speak about ending people's lives with such little regard.

"Sorry if I'm upsetting you, Fred." He truly sounded like he meant it. "I promised you I'd be honest."

I took another sip of hot chocolate and stroked over Watson's back. I didn't need the list. It wouldn't do any good. That was what I needed to focus on. The past was done, the future? Not so much. "Who else in Estes is part of the Irons crime family?"

He shook his head, almost regretfully. "That's one of those that I'll have to answer with the disclaimer. I won't tell you that. And... to a large degree, can't. As you can imagine, most of it's on a need-to-know basis. For all I know, *you* could be working with them." He hurried on when I flinched. "I know you're not, but you see my point."

I didn't push. I knew he wouldn't tell me, but he'd confirmed what Paulie had said. They were still here, just cloaked. I'd known the organization was large from the few things Dad had mentioned when he'd been investigating them, but I'd assumed they'd been local to the Kansas City area. Clearly, they were much bigger than I'd figured. But... how big?

He kept going, not waiting for another question. "I don't know if it matters to you or not, but I'm no longer part of the Irons family."

That threw me off. "You're not?"

He gave a snort of a laugh that made it seem like he felt it should have been obvious. "No, Fred. I killed Briggs, and Etta." He shrugged again. "Granted, she wasn't a big deal, but Briggs was. I have a price on my head now."

That hadn't entered my thoughts all week. Not once. That he'd have a price to pay for sparing my life. As he stared at me, I wondered if I was supposed to thank him. I couldn't make myself. If he wanted me to feel guilty or indebted, I wasn't going to.

But then, when I thought of how it could've gone down, I did feel indebted. And when I met his eyes, I meant every word I said with *every* ounce of my being. "Thank you for that. For sparing Watson, Leo, Katie, and Paulie."

He cocked an eyebrow. "And yourself?"

For whatever reason, I couldn't respond to that.

Strangely, that seemed to please him as his smile broadened. "You're ever Winifred Page, aren't you?" He stood, setting his hot chocolate aside, then moved toward the couch.

Watson lifted his head, growled, and bared his fangs.

Branson held up his hands. "Always safe, little man. Remember?"

I laid a reassuring hand on Watson's back. Though he hid his fangs once more, the rumble never left his chest, nor did his head return to my lap. He stayed focused on Branson, who sat beside us on the couch.

"And that brings me to why I'm here. Why I wanted to see you again."

"What does? The fact that you displeased the Irons family?"

"No." Branson reached for my hand but pulled back, reconsidering. "Come with me. Please."

I gaped at him. I hadn't seen that coming.

Still his eyes met mine, but they shifted, allowing me to fully see into him. See the hope, to see the inevitable hurt he knew would come.

"I don't even know your real name." I'd done a search on him many times throughout the week, and only found enough to realize Branson Wexler never existed. "And you want me to go away with you?"

"Branson Wexler isn't my real name—you're right. But if you choose to go with me, I'll tell you." He rushed on before I could respond. "Watson can come too, of course. I would never ask you to leave him behind. My feelings for you weren't ever a lie. I think you know that. I love you. I didn't expect someone like you to show up. Honestly, I didn't even want anyone. I had no desire to fall in love, but..." Another shrug. "But I did."

The voice of that middle school girl in the back of my mind joined with the refrain I'd heard from so many of the townspeople over the last several months. Asking me if I was crazy. How a woman like me could turn down a man like him. As they marveled, sometimes right to my face, about what was wrong with him that he could want me. As they threw metaphysical stones, telling me I thought too much of myself and that he deserved someone better. That cacophony shouted at me to ask why. Demand the list of reasons why in the world he loved me.

I shoved that aside. I was *not* a middle school child. And I'd heard all those voices before during my divorce—that somehow it had been my fault, that I needed to give him a second chance, and who was I to think I was good enough to say no.

Reaching over Watson, *I* took Branson's hand. "No."

Genuine pain flashed behind his eyes and then covered his face. He lifted my hand to his lips, pressed a kiss, and closed his eyes. When he lowered my hand and met my gaze once more, the pain and disappointment slid away behind his perfect exterior. "I knew you'd say that." His thumb smoothed over my knuckles. "You have a standing invitation, if you ever change your mind."

Strangely, affection for him flooded through me. For the friend I'd found in him in the beginning, and then the spark of heat that had ignited. "I won't change my mind. I don't want you to hold out hope for—"

"Let me take care of me, okay." He smiled gently, kissed my hand again, and released it before standing once more. "You're an amazing woman, Winifred Page. I regret any ounce of hurt I've caused you."

I had an impulse to stand, to pull him to me in a goodbye embrace. I didn't. But when I spoke, I held his gaze and allowed him to see into my eyes as he'd done to me. "Goodbye, Branson."

"See you later, Fred." He nodded at Watson. "I know I don't have to tell you, but take care of your mama." With that, he turned and left the way he'd snuck in.

There was a click of the back door. He even paused to relock it, which made me smile.

I knew the right thing to do was to call the police,

let Officer Green, or Officer Jackson, or whoever answered the phone, know that a fugitive was making his way out of town. I wasn't even tempted to make that call. I wasn't sure if it was because I was certain they didn't have a chance of catching him, or if it was because I was grateful he had spared our lives. Or maybe... just because he was Branson.

Exhaustion swept over me, and for the first time in a week, it wasn't unpleasant.

I stood and finished what I'd planned on doing the entire time. I got into my nightgown, turned down the bed, dimmed the lights except for the Christmas tree, and moved what remained of my hot chocolate next to Branson's on the side table.

"I know you're going to hate me for this, but give your mamma a little gift, okay?" Without waiting for permission, I scooped Watson into my arms and settled myself in the armchair. I didn't have it in me to read, so I sat by the crackling fire, Watson heavy on my lap, only squirming occasionally, and I stared out past the twinkling Christmas tree to the snow that had begun to fall over the trees once more.

Katie's Garlic Infused Bread recipe provided by:

2716 Welton St Denver, CO 80205
(720) 708-3026

Click the links for more Rolling Pin deliciousness:

RollingPinBakeshop.com

Rolling Pin Facebook Page

KATIE'S GARLIC INFUSED ARTISAN BREAD RECIPE

First Step:

Garlic

3 ounces garlic cloves, coated in olive oil and roasted in 350 degree oven until tender. Set aside.

Second Step:

1 ounce active dry yeast

20 ounces (2 1/2 cups) warm water

Place yeast and water in mixing bowl to activate the yeast.

Third Step:

Add-

2 pounds 11 ounces bread flour

10 ounces warm water

1 ounce salt

2 ounces olive oil

With dough hook, knead on low speed for 10 to 20 minutes.

Add roasted garlic after about 10 minutes.

Fourth Step:

Place in greased bowl, cover loosely with plastic wrap, and put in a warm place.

After dough doubles in size, punch down and turn out onto flour-covered surface.

Fifth Step:

Cut into 5 - 1 pound pieces.

Roll each piece with both hands to form a ball. Place on baking parchment-lined sheet pans dusted with flour and cover with plastic wrap for 30 to 45 minutes.

Sixth Step:

Remove plastic wrap and let sit for another 10 to 15 minutes.

Seventh Step:

When ready to put in oven, dust top of each

round loaf with flour, and with very sharp knife, score the top of each loaf.

Bake in 400 degree oven for 15 to 20 minutes or until dark golden brown. Should have a hollow sound when tapped.

AUTHOR NOTE

Dear Reader:

Thank you so much for reading *Wicked Wildlife*. If you enjoyed Fred and Watson's adventure, I would greatly appreciate a review on Amazon and Goodreads. Please drop me a note on Facebook or on my website (MildredAbbott.com) whenever you'd like. I'd love to hear from you.

I also wanted to mention the elephant in the room... or the over-sugared corgi, as it were. Watson's personality is based around one of my own corgis, Alastair. He's the sweetest little guy in the world, and, like Watson, is a bit of a grump. Also, like Watson (and every other corgi to grace the world with their presence), he lives for food. In the Cozy

Corgi series, I'm giving Alastair the life of his dreams through Watson. Just like I don't spend my weekends solving murders, neither does he spend his days snacking on scones and unending dog treats. But in the books? Well, we both get to live out our fantasies. If you are a corgi parent, you already know your little angel shouldn't truly have free rein of the pastry case, but you can read them snippets of Watson's life for a pleasant bedtime fantasy.

And don't miss book nine, *Malevolent Magic* coming November 2018, just in time for Christmas.

Much love, Mildred

PS: I'd also love it if you signed up for my newsletter. That way you'll never miss a new release. You won't hear from me more than once a month, nobody needs that many newsletters!

Newsletter link: Mildred Abbott Newsletter Signup

ACKNOWLEDGMENTS

A special thanks to Agatha Frost, who gave her blessing and her wisdom. If you haven't already, you simply MUST read Agatha's Peridale Cafe Cozy Mystery series. They are absolute perfection.

The biggest and most heartfelt gratitude to Katie Pizzolato, for her belief in my writing career and being the inspiration for the character of the same name in this series. Thanks to you, Katie, our beloved baker, has completely stolen both mine and Fred's heart!

Desi, I couldn't imagine an adventure without you by my side. A.J. Corza, you have given me the corgi covers of my dreams. A huge, huge thank you to all of the lovely souls who proofread the ARC versions and helped me look somewhat literate (in completely random order): Melissa Brus, Cinnamon, Ron Perry, Rob Andresen-Tenace, Anita Ford, TL Travis, Victoria Smiser, Lucy Campbell, Sue Paulsen, Bernadette Ould, Lisa Jackson, Gloria Lakritz, and Dennis Quinonez. Thank you all, so very, very much!

Kendra Prince, thank you for helping me chose the name Nadiya.

Marilee Stevens Woodrow, thank you for naming Etta Squire.

A further and special thanks to some of my dear readers and friends who support my passion: Andrea Johnson, Fiona Wilson, Katie Pizzolato, Maggie Johnson, Marcia Gleason, Rob Andresen- Tenace, Robert Winter, Jason R., Victoria Smiser, Kristi Browning, and those of you who wanted to remain anonymous. You make a huge, huge difference in my life and in my ability to continue to write. I'm humbled and grateful beyond belief! So much love to you all!

Made in the USA
Lexington, KY
05 November 2018